FROM THE WINDOW

FROM THE WINDOW

Keith Collins

Book Guild Publishing
Sussex, England

MORAY COUNCIL LIBRARIES & INFO.SERVICES	
20 20 85 69	
Askews	
_f_	

First published in Great Britain in 2007 by
Book Guild Publishing
Pavilion View
19 New Road
East Sussex BN1 1UF

Copyright © Keith Collins 2007

The right of Keith Collins to be identified as the author of this
work has been asserted by him in accordance with the
Copyright, Designs and Patents Act 1988.

All rights reserved. No part of this publication may be
reproduced, transmitted, or stored in a retrieval system, in any
form or by any means, without permission in writing from the
publisher, nor be otherwise circulated in any form of binding
or cover other than that in which it is published and without a
similar condition being imposed on the subsequent purchaser.

All characters in this publication are fictitious and any resemblance
to real people, alive or dead, is purely coincidental.

Typesetting in Baskerville by
Keyboard Services, Luton, Bedfordshire

Printed in Great Britain by
CPI Bath

A catalogue record for this book is available from
The British Library

ISBN 978 1 84624 089 8

I dedicate this book to my wife Janet and her friend Sylvia. Without their combined insistence this story would be gathering dust in the back of a drawer somewhere.

1

I sit looking out of the window of my third-floor apartment. The trees that line the road are just coming into leaf, and the pavements are shining with the moisture from the light overnight rain. Traffic will soon begin to build up as another day's work calls them from their homes. People walking to their jobs in town have already begun to appear, dressed in lightweight coats in case the rain returns. Most are walking on their own, but some walk in pairs, talking as they go. In the distance I can see a line of people forming up at a bus stop; it will not be long before the bus picks them up and deposits them in the centre of town, then the line will start to build up again. Later it will be mothers with their small children on the way to school, the children jumping in the small puddles on the pavement and the mothers trying to stop them. Everything looks normal for the start of a new day, but I wonder when or if I shall ever be able to join them again.

Soon the telephone will ring. It will be Allen, who has been my personal secretary for three years. He is always in the office early, at least a quarter of an hour before anyone else. He will ask for the schedule for the day, even though he could run the office just as well without me. I have already downloaded all the information from the computer, which he forwarded to me yesterday. And as always, all that's left for me to do is say yes, but it will be the same tomorrow and the day after that. Tonight

1

he will deliver to the door anything that he thinks I need to look through, and any household shopping that I have asked for. Clothing and personal items that I need are ordered from mail order catalogues and delivered to Allen's address. He will pass them on to me when they arrive.

It has now been almost six months since I have ventured into the outside world. And try as I will, the memory of the two men who molested me will not go away, even though they were caught and taken to court. The judge who sentenced them made a mockery of the justice system: they were both given jail sentences, but because of the time spent behind bars up to the time of getting to court, and allowing time off for good behaviour, they will be back on the streets in just under three years' time.

All the medical tests and police interviews that I had to undergo – then having to face both of the men in court – then their solicitor's accusations that I was as much to blame as the defendants, which was a blatant lie. My solicitor told me that the defence counsel would try to make it look that I was part to blame; even though they knew it was in no way my fault, they were working for the defendants and would try to show them in the best light. After the verdict the defendants did not argue with the sentence – in fact, they looked pleased with it. I was left feeling used and abused, with nowhere to go but here. The fear is that in a short while the two men will be out, living not far from where I had worked so hard to build up a good business.

The phone rings. I look at the clock and pick up the receiver, and as usual at this time in the morning, it's Allen.

'Hi, Jack, I hope you had a good night.' (My name is Jackie North, but Allen has always called me Jack.) 'Anything you require from the supermarket today, or anything from the shops?'

2

'No thanks, Allen, but there will be a small list tomorrow.'

'There are a few items in the post that should be looked at. I'll drop them off tonight after work.' We then go over the schedules for the day, to which I have little to add.

'Are you going out tonight, Allen?'

'No, I was thinking of having a night in and clearing the debris in the flat; it looks like a bomb's dropped. But what's on your mind? You sound as though you need something done.'

'Would you pick up a couple of takeaways on the way over and join me for a meal this evening? There is something I would like to ask you.' (This is a first.)

'I'll be there just after six, so get the kettle on.'

Allen sounds happy at the prospect of coming over tonight, but he cannot know how hard it has been to ask him. I have not met anyone face to face for six months, but now I have made a decision and I need to talk the first part of it over and need help to put it into practice and start the ball rolling.

Now I have to sit and wait until evening.

Until then I will tell you about myself.

2

I was adopted when I was only a few weeks old, so I never had any memories of my natural mother. I always thought of the couple who took me into their life as my parents. When I came to them I just had the name of Jackie; they gave me their surname of North, and now I can think of myself as nobody else, even though they told me that my real mother was still alive, and they had tried to find her in case I wanted to contact her in later life.

Daddy ran his own import and export company, and worked very hard. The returns were good and I never wanted for anything. Mum looked after me and the house; although they could afford help about the house, Mum seemed to do everything except the gardening: a retired postman used to come in a few days a week to keep things tidy. We called him 'Postie', and as I grew up I spent many happy hours in the garden with him. He prepared a small patch of ground for me when I was three, and told me that it was mine.

With Postie's help I planted seeds. I looked each day until the little green shoots were showing above the ground in straight rows. Postie said I must keep the ground clean and weed-free, and he showed me how to look after them. In those early years Postie taught me more about the way the world feeds its people and the way we must look after the land we live on than most people learn in a lifetime.

The day when the first flowers came into bud I could hardly wait to pick them. Postie said to wait a little longer for the petals to open, then we would be able to see the full glory of the blooms. He told me that they were wallflowers and the scent they would give off would be wonderful. Each day I would look; gradually the petals opened, and one day Postie said they were ready to cut and take indoors. He produced a pair of heavy scissors and showed me where to cut. Then he found some other greenery to put with them. After tying them loosely with raffia I was told they were ready to take to Mum.

When I walked into the kitchen where Mum was preparing our evening meal, I was the proudest little girl in the world. I handed the flowers to Mum and said, 'I have grown these especially for you, and Postie says they are now ready.'

When she looked at them tears started to stream down her face. I did not know what to do, I just said that I thought they would make her happy and that I was sorry they had made her cry. She took the flowers from me and placed them on the table. We sat on the floor and she told me to sit on her lap. Holding me really close she told me that these tears were tears of happiness, and that my gift was the best she had ever received. She hoped that one day I would receive such a gift: one I would remember for the rest of my life.

The phone rings again. I am not expecting a call. I let it ring for a few moments before picking up. When I do, I hear Allen's voice.

'Jack, I was beginning to think you had gone out somewhere.'

'Allen, what's the matter? Why are you ringing at this time of day? Something must be wrong.'

Allen's very gentle voice says, 'I am only ringing to confirm the arrangements for tonight. Only it took me by surprise this morning, and I am just checking to make sure I have got it right.'

'If you come with no food I won't let you in, otherwise I expect you soon after six.'

'That's great – see you then.'

Until I was five and started school, the time was spent with Mum during the day. She never seemed to be teaching me, but before I started school I knew how to cook simple things and look after the house. It all seemed like a game to me: everything we did seemed to be a game we played together. If we were making the beds or dusting the dining room it was all made into a game. All the time I was learning how to live a good and useful life.

Although Daddy worked hard, he always found time in the evenings to sit with me on his lap and read me stories. Some were from books with pictures in them and the writing was in large letters. He would read the lines then tell me to repeat them; as I did, he would point to the words that I was saying. It was not long before I was reading the words before Daddy had pointed to them. Again it did not feel that I was being taught, it was something that made me happy to do. It was the same with numbers, which were all made into games; if I did not get the answer right first time he would laugh and show me a different way to tackle the problem. When the time came to start school, the learning process was already well under way, although at that time I did not know it.

The first school I attended was St Mary's, a small private girls' school close to home, which was in Wallingford in Oxfordshire. The classes were small and we were expected to work hard, but I was happy there. A lot of the things we were being taught were the same as Mum and Daddy, not forgetting Postie, had been teaching me for years. It was not long before I found myself at the top of the class. Most of the others worked hard to catch up, but still classed me as a friend. At an early age I found myself helping others to keep up with the work we were doing. One or two would try to do me down but Daddy said it was not them, but they were only repeating what their parents had said. I was to take no notice of them at all, just keep on with the good work I had started and help as many of the others that wanted help.

At the age of eleven I went to a boarding school, Ralston Grange, but I was able to return home for weekends. For the first year I found it hard to adjust to being away: I missed Daddy and Mum more than I thought possible, and could not wait for the weekend to come so I could be home with them and sleep in my own room.

I found that Postie was working less in the garden as he grew older, and of course he did not come at all at weekends. He was a lovely man, and I missed him terribly. But after a few weeks he started to come round to the house on Saturday mornings especially to see me. We would sit in the garden and talk about school and the little plot of land that I still tried to look after.

It was some time before my interest in schoolwork returned. Then I realized that Mum, Daddy and Postie were always waiting for me at weekends. My grades began to improve with the sustained input I was giving, and again I was always in the top five in most subjects.

When I was thirteen and home for the long summer holidays, Mum and Daddy planned a two-week holiday to the south of France. Postie came to see me and we spent time sitting in the garden talking and drinking mugs of tea. When he left he said he hoped we would enjoy our holiday and would see us when we returned. Little did I know that was the last time I would ever see him. Two days later he suffered a heart attack and he never recovered. It was the blackest day of my life. I said to Mum and Daddy that we could not go to France now, we must stay and attend the funeral. They agreed and the holiday was cancelled. This was the first time death had ever touched my world, but it prepared me for events in the future. We stayed at home that holiday and worked in the garden as a mark of respect to Postie.

Returning to school, I was determined to work even harder. I wanted to get top grades in as many subjects as possible. I took extra tuition in the evenings and would take work home with me on weekends and during holidays. One rainy Saturday afternoon I was sat in the dining room doing some maths revision, when Daddy came in and said he wanted to have a talk. Pulling a chair over next to me he sat down and began to study the work I was doing.

'Mum is worried about you,' he said, 'she is concerned by the amount of work you are doing. She thinks you need to find time for recreation and take a break from this never ending studying.'

I told him that as I was nearly seventeen exams were coming up soon, which would assure me a place at university. 'That's where I want to go, so the work has to be done.'

In his gentle way he put his arm round my shoulders. 'Will you make an exception tomorrow? Just to please Mum.'

'All right. Where shall we go?'

'Anywhere you like.'

'Let's go down to Sandbanks and walk along the beach. I don't mind if it's raining and I hope there is a gentle wind blowing.'

'If that's what you want, we will be on our way soon after eight-thirty in the morning.' He got up and left me to go back to Mum in the kitchen. But he was unable to hide the grin that stretched from ear to ear. It had not just been Mum who had been concerned, and it reminded me just how much I loved them both.

3

In the end I need not have worried about the exams, for my marks were more than enough to get me into the university of my choice, Oxford, to study Business Management, Social Studies, Accountancy and Modern Languages.

I asked Mum and Daddy if I could go to Africa to work with the children for six months before going to university. Daddy asked for the reason for me wanting to go.

'I want to give something back – I've been supported all my life and will continue to be for some time to come. There's a need out in Africa, and I want to help fill it in my own little way, even if it's only for six months.'

In the end Mum and Daddy said if that's what I wanted to do they would contact the different agencies and try to find a place for me.

I was offered a place in Ethiopia to help an English nurse and a French dietitian, who were running an orphanage for forty children two hundred miles south-west of Adis Abeba; I accepted straight away. Over the next few weeks everything was organized and I was soon on my way to Africa.

Ethiopia is very poor, and the road network at best is uncertain; where I was heading for, it was nonexistent. After joining up with the supply truck in Adis Abeba it took three days to get to the orphanage, bumping over rough roads and then dirt trails, leaving a cloud of dust in our wake.

When we arrived, all the people from the village and all the children came out to greet us. The English nurse, Kimberly Thornton, and the French dietitian, May Ellis, both dressed in shorts and sweatshirts, made me welcome. After putting the luggage I had brought with me into Kimberly's hut, my working life there started by helping to unload the supplies that the truck had brought and storing them in a large hut attached to May's sleeping quarters. May was the only person who dealt with food distribution, and kept a tight control over the stores. Next to the hut that I now occupied with Kimberly was the dispensary, which was her domain.

That evening Kimberly and May explained how things were run and the role that I would play there. I was pleased to find that we could all converse in both English and French; although my French was not as good as it could be, it was to improve over my time with them.

The orphanage consisted of two large huts, one for sleeping, the other for living and as a schoolroom. The ages of the forty children there ranged from six months to thirteen years. Kimberly said that the older ones could speak a halting form of English. She said I would soon get used to it but would find it difficult at first. It was going to be my task to help with the education and the hygiene of the children and their quarters. She laughed and said, 'At least your job's been made easier since the village has had a well; when we first got here, all the water had to be carried from a small river over a mile away.' For this I was grateful, as the thought of transporting water for forty children was not a pleasant one.

Next day very little was done, as the children were excited because I was a new face. I was apprehensive because of my lack of knowledge. Most of the children were slim but not undernourished, as May had worked out a good balance between the amount of food they

11

required and the amount available. Before the end of the day I could understand some of the things they were saying, but they could not pronounce my name and soon I became Atta. And Atta I remained for the rest of my stay with them.

We started our days at six-thirty: I would wash the little ones and get them ready for the day, while Kimberly would check on those who were on medication and look at any other problems that had arisen. The first meal of the day would be light and May did the preparations for this herself. We all sat together at four tables in the living-cum-schoolroom, the older children and us feeding the little ones.

In less than a fortnight I was accepted as part of the family. The hours we worked were long, never finishing until the last ones were in bed, but the time flew by and the supply truck was there again, which meant that I had been there a month. With it came a letter from Mum and Daddy, who sent me all their news and wanted to know all about the orphanage. I had written a letter home and had it ready to go back with the supply truck: there was so much to tell them that I found it hard to find a place to stop. I was so pleased with their letter that it was put in my case and read many times over the next month.

I was always with the children, but the education they needed was far different to the education that I had grown up with. With the help of a man and his wife from the village we taught them the basic skills to survive in the hostile environment into which they had been born. The older ones seemed to look after the very young by natural instinct. If I was having trouble, one of them would always be there to give a helping hand. They brought home to me just how privileged my upbringing had been, because, like me, they had no idea who their natural parents were.

12

And yet they were happy, and I was positive they would grow to be useful members of their community.

As the months passed Kimberly and May became good friends to me; I shall never forget them or the dedication they gave to help those in need. As the time to return home came, I was sad to think I might never see them again. When the day came for me to leave, the children gathered and sang for me. The eldest came and handed me a roll of white paper. When it was rolled out, there was the right footprint of all the children that I had helped to look after; Kimberly had written their names over each one. The tears streamed down my face, and I remembered the flowers I had given to Mum and what she had told me.

4

When I arrived home Mum and Daddy were so pleased to see me, I thought they were going to burst. Mum said I had lost weight and Daddy told me how well I looked. For the next week we sat or walked and I told them of the life I had led for the last six months, about Kimberly and May and all the children. I showed them my parting present and reminded Mum of the flowers all those years ago, and again I saw a tear roll down her cheek.

It would not be long before I was off to university, and I started to put things to one side that I would need to take with me. Daddy drove me and Mum up to Oxford to look for somewhere for me to stay. Eventually we found a place about a mile from the university so I could cycle to classes. The lady who owned the house had a son of fourteen and had not long lost her husband. The room was not large but had its own bathroom, and I would have full use of the kitchen; I knew I would be happy there. Daddy told Mum and me to go and have a look around the neighbourhood while he sorted out the arrangements. Later we met up at the car and drove home.

When I arrived at the university for my first term students were running all over the place, none of whom seemed to know where they were supposed to be. I was doing well but still had a few places to find and forms to fill in. By the end of the day I must have walked miles, and after cycling back to my lodgings I was ready for a bath and a quiet sit down. I still had a bundle of forms and papers to read through and to sign and return in the morning.

Next morning I was in the kitchen tipping cereal into a bowl when Mrs Carter came in to make breakfast for her son. She said, 'You can sit in here with us, you know; there's no need to take your breakfast to your room to eat.'

The son, James, came in and sat opposite me. I looked at him and said, 'Good morning.'

'Morning.' He ate his breakfast and left the room without another word.

Mrs Carter sat down with a cup of tea. 'I noticed you went without a meal last night. That will not do; if you leave a note for what you want for your evening meal I can cook it with ours, and it will be ready for you when you get in at night.'

She said she only worked at the hospital from nine until three. 'I'm always home before James comes in from school, and a bit of extra cooking will be no trouble at all.'

I tried to say no, but she insisted and cooked the evening meal ever since. I think that Daddy had something to do with the arrangement.

The workload at university was heavy, and I found little time for social activities. I met a young man called David Hern, who was studying some of the same subjects as myself. He was the sort of man you did not look at twice, but he had a memory like a sponge. Although he did not like socializing and would shut up like a clam in company, in the end we became friends and would study together two or three times a week. Although his input was far more than mine, he never complained. At weekends we would walk by the river, occasionally going to the theatre. He never asked for anything other than friendship, and for this I was grateful, as I was not ready for a serious relationship with anyone.

In the early days James Carter was hard to get along with; he was withdrawn and appeared to hate the world and everyone in it. It was obvious he was missing his father and had turned in on himself. After having a word with his mother I began to try harder with him. It was months before we were really talking, but he eventually came round, and on some Sunday afternoons when the weather was good, he and his mother would accompany David and me for walks along the riverbank.

One evening James came to me and asked if I could help with some maths homework he was having trouble with. When we had finished he stayed and we talked. He told me how much he missed his father, and that he could not work out why it had to happen to their family. I had been waiting for him to say something, and now I told him how I started my life and of the wonderful people who had taken me in as their own daughter.

I said, 'I never knew who my real mother or father were, and I still can't find out who or where they were.'

James was looking at the floor, and I let him think for a little while. Then he said that he had his mother and had known his father, and would carry fond memories of him for the rest of his life.

I ended by saying, 'Although it's hard for you, I think you had a little bit better start than me. The best thing to do is to get on with your life; it's what your father would have wanted you to do.'

The next evening he put his head round my door, said 'Thanks' and then was gone. But it made my day.

When the exam results were listed at the end of my time at university, I had finished in the top four in all the subjects I had taken. David had finished top in nearly all his subjects, and I was pleased for him: he deserved every mark and had helped me gain many of mine. Like me, he was not certain what he would do; I still wonder what he is doing now. We had been good friends, but now I have lost contact with him. But I still get a Christmas card from Mrs Carter and James.

5

Looking out of the window and down the street I see the mothers and children returning home from school. There has been no more rain, and now the children are swinging their coats over their shoulders and holding onto their mothers' hands. I had not realized it was so late.

When Allen comes round tonight I want him to think that it's almost time for me to return to work. I am dressed and ready, and it feels good to be back in working clothes again, even if they are now a bit on the tight side.

After university I went back home to spend time with Mum and Daddy, and decide what I wanted to do with my life. Daddy was nearing sixty and was thinking of retiring and selling his business. He said he was sure he could use my learned expertise, and there would be a good chance I would be retained after he had sold the business to someone else.

I told him it would never work: he still thought of me as his little girl (which I was) and would be looking over my shoulder most of the time. Whoever took over from him would think I was there to spy, reporting back to him how things were going. I told him I wanted to do something that would help the general public as a whole, while earning enough to keep me. But I still had no idea in what direction to start looking.

Within days Daddy had brought home armfuls of

18

publications with places advertising positions that needed to be filled. It was three frustrating days before I found the type of job I was looking for, in Hospital Management. When the application came I read it through with Daddy, who said, 'It looks as though you are overqualified for the position.'

'It's better than taking on a role that I would struggle with; it looks as if there are prospects of promotion. Also the hospital is near enough so I can come home at weekends.'

Within days of sending off the application I was invited up to West Manston Hospital in London, which was on a sprawling site. The main building must have been built in the 19th century, with a mixture of more modern buildings built on and around it. As soon as I gave my name in at the main reception desk, I was taken to an office where two people were seated at desks reading through piles of paper. They introduced themselves and the interview began. A woman who was looking at the application form I had sent in started to ask questions. Although I was nervous, I was pleased with the way I handled myself.

After nearly a hour the man seated at the other desk asked, 'Is this the job you are really looking for? Given your qualifications, you should be looking for a position at a higher level.'

'I think it's wiser to start with something I feel I can do well. According to the information you sent me, there is ample opportunity for advancement.'

All he said was 'Very good,' and we were off for a tour of the hospital.

The next two hours were spent walking from place to place, with a running commentary of the work being done, finishing up in the administration block which also held the offices of the Hospital Management Team. The man then asked, 'What do you think now you've seen the place? Do you think you could fit in there?'

'Well, for the first month I'll get lost in the hallways and passages every time I leave the office. Apart from that, it's the sort of challenge I'm looking for.'

They thanked me for coming and said they would be in touch in the next few days.

It was almost a week before a letter with 'West Manston Hospital' printed on the back came. Taking it into the kitchen I told Mum that it had arrived. She said, 'Have you got the job?'

'I haven't opened it yet. Will you do it?'

Mum laughed but took the letter, tore it open and removed a single sheet of typed paper. She read it through, looked at me and said, 'It looks like they want you to start as soon as possible.' She gave me a big hug and we sat in the kitchen, where I could not stop talking. She said, 'There's still a lot to do, and we can start to sort things out when Daddy comes home.'

The first thing Daddy said was, 'If that's the case, you will need somewhere to live. Leave that to me, and you and Mum make a list of the things you'll need.'

Before the end of the week Daddy said he thought he had found something suitable, and we drove up on the Saturday morning to look at a small flat. When we found the place it was a large house with a nice garden. At some time a small granny annexe had been added to the back, and it was this we had come to look at. It consisted of a kitchen-cum-living room which was not a bad size, a small bedroom and a bathroom with a shower. It was furnished and carpeted, and we were told that this was included in the rent. There was an allotted car parking space, and the flat was within three miles of the hospital and on a bus route, so I could cycle or in bad weather travel on the bus. In fact, it was perfect and I could see myself living there already. Daddy left a deposit and said his solicitor would contact them on Monday to sort out the lease.

On the way home I pointed out, 'We haven't asked how much the rent is. I might not be able to afford to pay it.'

Daddy glanced at Mum. 'Don't worry about that yet. You get a few wage cheques put by, and then we can talk again.'

I did worry, though, because I knew Daddy was thinking of retiring, and I did not want to eat into their savings.

6

A fortnight later I was in the flat and working at West Manston. For the first month I seemed to be assisting others or being instructed by them, I was never sure which. Then I landed in the Accounts Department and was glad of my university training. Every day was a never-ending round of chasing or trying to raise more funds, not for new projects or equipment, but for the day-to-day running of the hospital. This was the task that I had been taken on to deal with, and it was much larger that I had first envisaged. Although I was not supposed to, I found myself taking work home to try to catch up with the backlog.

By the time I had been there for five months, I was beginning to get the filing system into order. But while trying to balance the money being spent with the money in hand, I had a shock. All the time we were running very near to a deficit, except in one account, out of which nothing was ever spent, there sat thousands of pounds doing nothing. It had been growing for over several years, but I did not know where it had come from. From the time I had been taking care of the accounts nothing had been added, except the interest of about 2 per cent.

In the end I found it: this was money that had been claimed back from VAT. But for some unknown reason my predecessor had put it into a separate account, and it had just been growing.

I called a meeting with the other members of the team

and asked what should be done with this money. I was told that if the money was put into the hospital running account, it might affect our central funding next year. And if there was no way of channelling it back undetected and closing the account, they had no suggestions as what to do. It was beyond me, so I said I would look into it further and get back to them.

The next weekend I went home and had a long talk to Daddy, who said, 'I don't like it – this could be a scam, or it could be an oversight. The first thing to do is to freeze the account so nothing can be removed from it until a solution is worked out.'

He gave me the name of a firm of accountants up in town who he knew well, and said he would get someone to give me a call. I told him he had taken a weight off of my mind, and looked forward to the call.

On the Tuesday morning I received a call from Wicks and Wicks Accountants. Mr Wicks sounded elderly and told me he had spoken to my father, who had outlined the problem. He suggested he should send one of his men to check things out for me. I asked if it could be done away from the hospital, as I wanted to be as discreet as possible. I suggested we look over documents at my flat. I was told the young man's name who would deal with it was Peter Backstone, and I made arrangements to meet him at seven on Thursday evening.

Wednesday and Thursday were spent collecting all the information I thought would be needed to find a way to move the money without causing any problems, and to find out if it was just an oversight or a means for someone to take the money without the hospital knowing.

Peter arrived early; in fact, he was there not long after I arrived home myself. He was thirty-two years old and very good looking, with a ready smile. Standing six feet tall with broad shoulders, and not an ounce of excess weight anywhere, he appeared to be the sort of man who was a regular at the gym or else ran or jogged daily.

Peter said he had eaten so I made coffee then we sat at the kitchen table and started going through the records I had brought from the hospital, with Peter feeding items into the laptop he had brought.

At nine o'clock he said he had all the information he needed. 'By the look of things, nobody has done anything wrong, but it's strange that a new account had been opened for the repayments. I'll work through the data I've taken, and will return tomorrow night with a solution to return the money to the hospital account that does not point a finger of suspicion at anybody.'

Looking from the window I can see Allen parking his car opposite the apartment block. Moments later the intercom cracks into life.

'If you would like to go through, dinner will be served in a few moments.'

I push the button to let him into the apartment block, and go to my door and open it, and stand waiting for him to climb to stairs. Carrying several carrier bags he comes walking down the hallway.

'Hello, Jack. You look good. Can I put this lot straight into the kitchen?'

'Yes.' As he walks to the kitchen I shut the door and follow him through.

'I know you like Indian food, so there is a selection here. Help yourself.'

Taking the plates from the warming drawer at the bottom of the cooker, we fill them from the boxes and take them into the dining room.

'If you find some glasses and an opener there is a nice little red wine to help this lot down, if you fancy some.'

I get the glasses and we sit down to eat, and I sip the wine he has brought.

'You've been missed at the office, you know; when can we expect you back? Soon? You can't spend the rest of your life up here; it's not healthy.'

'The office will have to wait a little longer, but I am getting out of condition, and that's why I asked you to come. The food's good, but it's not helping my size. I shall have to get a new wardrobe soon if things go on the way they have been going.'

Allen's so natural and finds no problem talking face to face with me after all this time. 'So how can I help? Your word is my command. Tell me how I can help, and I will see what I can do.'

Allen is a little overweight for his height, and I feel uncomfortable asking if he goes to a gym, because I want to go and need someone to accompany me for a start. He tells me, 'I tried it a couple of times about a year ago, but it didn't agree with me. After an hour working out and then walking back to the flat I had difficulty getting up the stairs, so I gave it up. But if that's what it takes to get you out and working again, I'll look for somewhere tomorrow. And I'd better shake out the tracksuit and throw the trainers in the washing machine.'

We sit at the table and talk until almost nine, when he says, 'I'm happy to stay longer, but don't you think this has been long enough for a start? I'll see if I can find a gym that's not too crowded and give you a ring tomorrow afternoon, and perhaps we can meet again to talk it over.'

We walk to the door, and he takes my hand in both of his. 'I'm very pleased to see you again.' And then he is gone.

Allen had been a male nurse but had become unhappy with his working environment. When I wanted more staff, he had been the first person I had hired and had proved

25

his worth time and time again. I consider him more of a friend than an employee. Now he is gone I can still feel the warmth of his hands on mine, and I realize just how much I have missed the outside world. I need to get back into it; there is much to do, and at last I have made a start. I sit down in the chair by the window and look down on the street; now the light from the street lamps is casting shadows, and it all looks different from the view in daylight.

The evening following the first meeting, Peter and I sat at the kitchen table and he talked me through what I should do. He had computer printouts and had prepared it all on disc so I could put all the data straight into the hospital computer. I understood what he had done, and it was a relief to know that it could all be accomplished without any repercussions. His explanation had only taken an hour and then we were finished and it was all packed up ready to take into work tomorrow. He said he had not eaten and suggested we go to the pub just round the corner and grab something to eat and a quick drink.

It was a large place split up into small alcoves, with tables for four or six people. We were given a table for four, and I sat one side and Peter sat opposite me. Although he looked extremely fit, his skin was very pale. It showed the many hours he spent in the confines of an office. His dark hair made his skin look even whiter than it really was. After ordering the food and a drink, he asked me about myself.

I said, 'There's not much to tell,' but before the end of the meal I had told him more about myself than I had ever told anybody. We ordered another drink and I said, 'Now it's your turn.'

He said his father had died when he was young and

he had been brought up by his mother. A family friend had managed to find him a position in a firm of accountants in his local town, and he learnt his trade while working there. He had heard that Wicks and Wicks dealt with large and complicated accounts, and when a position became vacant in the firm he applied and was accepted. Peter said it was a good way to learn more while still earning good money. He had been there almost three years, and although he liked the job he felt that he would be moving on in the near future, probably back to Swindon, where he was born. He said he would like to set up an office of his own, and he would be nearer to his mother, who was not in the best of health.

When we left the pub Peter walked me back to my flat. He said how much he had enjoyed the evening and when he left me at the door he kissed my cheek and said good night, and I watched as he walked off towards the underground station. When I got inside I did not know if I felt happy or sad; I was glad the problem at the hospital had been resolved, but sad to think that I might not see Peter again. After showering and getting into bed I spent most of the night thinking about him.

On Saturday I went home to see Mum and Daddy; I told him that my little problem had been sorted out and would be dealt with first thing Monday. I said Wicks and Wicks had been a great help, but never mentioned Peter.

On Monday morning I called the rest of our group into the conference room and laid out how the problem could be resolved. I did not tell them of the help received from Peter, as I thought they might not appreciate the fact that I had asked for outside help in a private matter. They all agreed it was the way to proceed, and I headed back to my office. In less than a hour it was all taken care of – a few phone calls to banks and the insertion of the data on the disc onto the hospital records – and

I could get back to the job I was suppose to be doing. As I was finishing the phone rang, and when I picked it up Peter was on the other end.

He said, 'I enjoyed the evening on Friday. Would you like to go out again on Wednesday, this time on me?'

My heart gave a jump and I said, 'That would be nice.'

'I'll pick you up about eight and we can go up to town.'

Although the office was very busy I found it hard to concentrate for the next two days, and on Wednesday I dressed in my best and took special care over the make-up; I had not been this excited for a long time.

Peter picked me up in a small two-seater MG sports car and showed me the way to get into it without showing too much leg. The meal was lovely and we talked about so many things, and afterwards we walked along the Thames and looked at the lights reflecting on the water. When we returned and parked outside my flat I asked if he would like a drink or maybe coffee. He leant over and kissed me on the mouth, then said, 'Maybe another night; I've an early start in the morning. Could I see you next week and take in a show?'

Again that night in bed I felt joy and disappointment. There were feelings I had not felt before, and I did not know how to respond to them. Each week after that he would pick me up and we would go out to dinner or a show. Peter was generous and never minded spending money. Wicks and Wicks must have paid good money because one night we went to his place, which was near the centre of town in a large new block of very upmarket apartments called Mid West Place. The furnishings were new and modern. We drank a little wine and listened to music. It was late and he asked, 'Would you like to stay the night?'

I said, 'I've never slept with a man before ... you might be disappointed if I do stay.' He picked me up like a feather and carried me into the bedroom. I told him not to put on the lights because I would feel better in the dark. Peter was a strong man but was gentle with me, and made me feel very special. The next morning I was the happiest woman in London.

After a year the workload at the hospital grew heavier by the week, and there never seemed to be enough money to pay the staff we needed; the projects that should have been finished were not even started; the staff were working long hours, and it showed. If things did not get better, we were in for a disaster sooner or later. Even one of our own department staff had left because of the demands put upon him; he knew that there was nothing he could do to help.

All this time I was meeting Peter at least once a week, most times staying at his apartment for the night. But he always went home at the weekends, usually on a Friday night and was not back until Monday morning. I thought it strange that he never invited me to go down with him; I surmised that this was because his mother was still not well, so I never asked to go.

One evening we had been watching a film on the TV. When it finished the news came on; they were talking about the shortages in the country's hospitals. I asked Peter for some paper and a pen so I could jot a few things down, things that I knew were happening at our own hospital. He reached under a low table and gave me some paper, and found a pen on a bookcase behind me. I wrote about half a page and folded it to go into my bag to read again at work tomorrow.

7

My colleagues and I were now going in early each day to try to keep up with the problems now facing the hospital, and most of us were there long after our official hours. When Peter rang the next week I cried off, saying I was so tired and needed a good night's sleep. I heard the disappointment in his voice but he said he would ring later. It was the Friday of the following week when I realized Peter had not been in touch again. I rang Wicks and Wicks and asked to be put through to him; I wanted to apologize for my long silence.

The girl on the switchboard said, 'He's left and gone back home.'

'Has his mother taken a turn for the worse? When do you expect him back?'

'No,' she said, 'he cleared his office earlier in the week and returned to Cheltenham. I think he's going into his father's construction business.'

My head started spinning and I had difficulty breathing; there were questions to ask, but the words would not come. After a while the girl on the other end said, 'Are you still there?'

'Yes; can you give me a phone number where he can be contacted?'

'I'm not allowed to give out that information. Ring back next week when the regular operator will be back – I'm only here temporarily because of holidays.'

I replaced the receiver and sat with tears streaming

down my face. I could not stop shaking. I picked up my coat and bag and walked out of the office without saying a word to anyone. I needed to get home, so I headed for the railway station, not even going back to the flat.

Mum and Daddy were surprised to see me home so soon, but knew something was wrong as soon as I walked in. I was in tears again as soon as I saw them. Mum sat me down and put her arms around me and asked, 'What on earth is the matter?' Daddy sat in his usual chair and listened while I told my sorry story.

When I finished I said, 'You must think me a fool, but I had no idea. He was the first man I've ever loved, and now I don't know what to do.'

Daddy got up and told me to stay with Mum, 'There's someone I have to talk to,' and then left the room. When he returned half an hour later, he looked grave. I was still with Mum and he pulled his chair over so he could be closer to me.

He said, 'There's no easy way to say what has to be said; let me finish before you ask anything. Peter has indeed gone home to Cheltenham, which is the headquarters of Mid West Construction, owned by his father. It's a multi-million-pound company, building not only in this country but overseas as well. His mother and father are very active. His father sent Peter to Wicks and Wicks to gain experience in accountancy, as Wicks and Wicks are the accountants for Mid West Construction. While he was there he received no salary, only an allowance from his father. And the apartment he stayed in belonged to the company, so he never paid any rent all the time he was there.

'But there's worse to come. Peter does not live with his parents; he is with his wife and son who is aged three. They live two miles from his parents' home, and when he was staying in London he went home to them every weekend. He has known for months when he would be leaving London.'

I sat there in total shock, holding Mum's hand and looking at the floor. All those lies – he had started telling them from the moment we had met and continued right up to the last. I wanted to kill him.

Daddy said, 'There's not much we can do; we could tell his wife but that would only ruin her life as well. I don't think you want to do that to someone who is as innocent as you are.'

In the end I told them I would leave it (but there was no way I was going to forget). Poor Mum never said a word at the time, but she gave me the strength to get on with my life by just being there.

On Sunday I called the hospital and told them that I was not well and would be back later in the week. I asked Daddy, 'How did you find the information about Peter so quickly?'

'I rang Wicks senior at his home; he's been my accountant for years, and my friend for a very long time.' I suddenly realized how little I knew about his working life. I knew he was in import and exports, but that was as far as it went.

I told him that, 'As I'm going to be home for a few days, will you take me to your office for the day?'

'Let's go on Monday.'

I did not know what to expect, but we drew up in front of a large office block in Oxford and parked in a named parking place. The building was not new but looked as though it had been built in the late Forties. When we entered through the glass doors at the front I found myself in a large reception area, with a desk manned by two secretaries. As we approached one looked up and said,

32

'Good morning Mr North, coffee and the morning mail will be in your office in a few minutes.'

Daddy said, 'Thanks Jill, but would you make that two cups?' and we headed for the lift. He explained that his offices consisted of the ground and first floor. The rest of the floors were accessed from other sides of the building and occupied by other companies.

We walked out of the lift into a huge room filled with desks and computers; the sound of the phones never stopped. Daddy took me to his office, which was large but plainly furnished with comfortable furniture. This was where he had spent years of his life, and I never dreamed it was such a large operation.

'Do all the people outside work for you?'

'Yes, and there are more in other rooms downstairs. All they do there is move paper and words around the world. But those words enabled people to move thousands of tons of every commodity you can think of, from any pick-up point to any destination you care to name. There are a few exceptions, such as firearm and munitions, and we don't handle livestock or nuclear materials. But everything else that needs moving we move, always trying our best to get it there on time. Our job is to see that the transport is where it's supposed to be when the consignment is ready for collection, and that all the clearances and export documents are in order. And then when it arrives at its destination, all import documents have to be in order for the cargo to be landed. It all sounds easy, but it takes a lot of people who know what they are doing to get it right.'

I spent the rest of the morning walking around the offices and talking to the staff – when they were not on the phone or running from one place to another. It all showed Daddy in a new light and taught me I must switch off when away from the office and never to take work home, even when things were getting behind. It brought home to me that I had never seen Daddy with his work at home, and never heard him talking business on the phone. When he was home he was there for Mum and me.

When I awake and look at the bedside clock I realize I have overslept. I must get moving or Allen will be on the phone before I have read the computer mail this morning. Sitting in my dressing gown in front of the computer I find nothing that Allen will need my help with. The phone rings just as I finish reading.

'Morning, Jack. You OK this morning?'

'Everything is fine, and there are no problems your end as far as I can see. But it is nearing the end of the month and if you send through the figures I can start sending out the accounts.'

'That's right, keep the bank manager happy and the bailiffs from the door. I'll send it all through to you as soon as possible, but in the meantime is there anything you want me to collect for you?'

'There is nothing I really want today, but if you find a gym that we can use, come and see me again tonight.'

After a short intake of breath he says, 'That's great; so if all goes well I will be round the same time tonight, so get the kettle on.' With that the phone goes dead and once again I am left with nothing to do.

I sit in front of the window again and see a better morning. There is a hazy light, but the sun will break through later. The mums taking the small children to school will not need their coats or umbrellas.

At half past one Daddy took me for lunch at a pub about

34

ten minutes walk from the office. While we were eating he asked, 'What do you think of my little empire?'

I said, 'I'm amazed at how large a concern it is – why have you never brought me to the office before?'

'When you wanted to see it all, I knew you would ask. But it won't be mine for much longer. This is in strictest confidence and must not go any further – at this moment I am in negotiations with some very big players, and if all goes well I will retire in less than three months.'

'Is that what you really want? Do you think that you can live without the stress of the day-to-day running of such a big outfit?'

'Believe it or not, I'm over sixty, and all I need now is to be home with Mum and keep an eye on you. And I say that in the nicest sense possible.'

I spent the next day at home with Mum, who told me that I was in no way to blame for the things that had happened, and that I should always remember that not all men were like Daddy. I asked if she knew how Daddy spent his working day. She smiled and said, 'If anything happens that he can't handle, he'll be straight home to tell me. But in all the years we've been married that has not happened once.'

The long weekend had been good, and I felt that I could go back into the outside world again, knowing that there was always home to go to if things went wrong. I rang the hospital and let them know I would be back to work the next morning.

For the next six months I worked even harder than I had before. The hurt I felt over the experience with Peter eased a little, but the memory would not go away. Then we lost another member of our staff and it looked as though he would not be replaced. Every department in the hospital was short of staff. It was always the same: either the wages were not enough or the skilled staff needed for the top posts could not be found. Most of the time we were trying to get more and more funding just to keep our heads above water.

8

That weekend I talked over the things that were happening at the hospital with Daddy. He seemed to be in a good mood and so was Mum. I asked, 'What's going on?'

Daddy said, 'There is something we have to tell you. I was going to tell you as soon as you got home, but you haven't given me a chance. As from yesterday I am retired; the sale of the company went through and I received payment yesterday. I cleared my desk, and now Mum and I are going to see some of the places I have been dealing with for the past thirty years. But from now on, we shall be strictly tourists.'

I kissed them both and wished them all the happiness they both deserved. It was quite obvious that they were happy with the idea of retirement.

Daddy said, 'I've just made a big decision in my life, and now I think it's time you do the same. I've been listening to you over several months, and I think what's needed is a central register of all hospital personnel: somewhere any hospital can call if they can't find the type of staff they're looking for. This could also include the staffing of doctors' surgeries. It'll be a big undertaking, and you'll need some staff to help. Now I have the time I can help setting up the enterprise – and I've just been given a nice big cheque, and can finance the business until it is on its feet.'

I said, 'I wouldn't know where to start. There are hundreds of job classifications and thousands of personnel, and that's if I were to only list those in the south of England.'

Daddy said, 'If you start with the lowliest positions and work your way up, the top people will be knocking on your door before you know it.'

My mind was going in all directions at once; the need was there, but the cost of setting it all up would run into thousands of pounds.

None of us did anything that weekend but talk about what Daddy had suggested. On Sunday night Mum and Daddy drove me back up to London.

I said, 'I need a week to think through all that we've discussed over the weekend. If I can sort it out in my own mind, there'll be an answer next Friday night.'

Daddy said, 'There is a little secret I've been keeping to myself. Mum and I are flying out to Amsterdam tomorrow morning, and we shall stay there for a few days. It's a little present for me as much as anything else – I've always wanted to look around the Van Gogh museum, and now I have the time we are on our way.'

I kissed them both and wished them a lovely time, then stood in the street and watched the car tail light until they were gone.

Although it was the same hectic round at work the following week, I did find the time to look at the hospital records for the personnel that worked on the site. There were thirteen hundred in total, and almost eight hundred of those had some medical knowledge. Next was the records of all those who had left our employment in the last year, and their reason for leaving. It gave me some idea of the task that lay ahead if I decided to take Daddy's advice.

By Thursday I could not wait, and so at lunchtime I

phoned home to see if Mum and Daddy were back from Holland. Mum answered the phone.

'We arrived back on Wednesday evening. We enjoyed ourselves – we spent one complete day in the museum, and Daddy has spoken of nothing else since. Of course, we had to do a little shopping as well.' Then she passed me over to Daddy.

I said, 'I suppose you have brought the "Sunflowers" home with you.'

'I would have brought them all home if they had given me the chance. That man may have been mad, but he was the most talented madman there has ever been. The colours just jump out at you, and then when he was in his black period, the paintings showed you the inside of the man's mind. I have seen some of his work that is not on public display, but that hadn't prepared me for the day we spent in the museum.'

This was a side of Daddy I never knew about: we had nice pictures about our home, but not even one reproduction of anything by the great man.

In the end Daddy said, 'But this isn't the reason for your call; you've come to a decision.'

'I've thought of nothing else for the whole week, and I've done quite a bit of research into the project. It'll be a long-term project, and it may take two years before there will be any significant returns. But it looks as though it can be a very viable undertaking, and one for which there is a great need. The big problem is that I'm going to need a lot of help to set it up. And I don't think that's fair on you; after all, you have just retired and should be enjoying your time with Mum.'

'Don't you worry your head about that. Just hand in your notice, which I presume will be a month, and we will talk some more at the weekend.'

The next day I handed in my resignation to the head

39

of our department, explaining to him my reasons for leaving.

He said, 'There are agencies that offer some of this type of information, but they don't provide or hold a comprehensive record of hospital staff. Do you have any idea how big a task you are proposing to take on, and how long it will be before you can offer your services to hospitals and clinics?'

I said, 'I will have some very professional business advice, and I am willing to work hard to get it all running. Would you write me a letter of introduction to other hospitals? Not only will I be offering them my services, but I also need to know the number of staff working there, the qualifications they hold and what positions they found most difficult to fill.'

'Rather you than me, but I will see what I can do. I can have a talk to the legal boys as to what information you are likely to be able to ask for and receive.'

I went home on Friday night rather than sitting on my own until Saturday. Daddy said, 'Tonight we go out and celebrate, everything else can wait until tomorrow. Go and have a shower and put on your best dress; we'll go to Oxford and have a good meal.'

The drive to Oxford did not take long, and Mum and Daddy were quiet for most of the way, but I noticed that they kept glancing at one another. When we entered the restaurant it was more than half full; we were shown to our table and Daddy ordered drinks. It was all very plush, with thick carpets and a piano playing at the far end of the room. Mum was fiddling with something on her lap, and when she raised her hand to pick up her glass, there was the most beautiful diamond ring I had ever seen.

She gave me her hand. 'Daddy bought it for me while we were in Holland. He told me it was just for being me;

I hope he is not going soft in the head. Who else does he think I could be?'

Daddy pushed a little blue box across the table and said, 'Here is a little something for you.'

When I opened the box there was a polished gold cross with a diamond mounted in the centre, suspended on a fine gold chain. Daddy said, 'That's just for being you; I can't think of another man that's been so lucky for so long.'

I got up and went around the table and kissed them both. Then Daddy fastened the cross around my neck and told me I was the best thing that had ever happened to them. I cannot remember the meal, but it was another evening to remember for the rest of my life.

Saturday and Sunday were spent in the dining room, making what seemed to be endless lists of things that would be needed to set the enterprise up. And by Sunday night I began to realize the costs that would be involved. Daddy just said, 'The financial side is for me to sort out, and you're not to worry about it. I'll be with you all the way for the first six months anyway, that's if you could put up with me. I'd expect to see a little income by then, although it'll be probably be two years before it is fully operational.'

After that I phoned home every night to discuss the things that had been thought of during the day, and compare notes. Two weeks later Daddy said he had found an office which he thought would be just right to start with; it was on the outskirts of Oxford and could easily be reached from home. He said we could go and view at the weekend, and if I thought it suitable, he could then start getting things put into place.

9

When I got home on Friday night there was a strange car parked in the drive. I thought that there must be visitors, so I went around the side of the house and in through the kitchen door, where I found Mum busy with the evening meal. I put my overnight bag on the floor and asked if there was anything I could do to help. She said, 'No thanks, you go and have your shower and change, but first go and see Daddy; he is in the study.'

When I walked in I was surprised to find him in there alone. I asked where the visitor was.

'Oh yes,' he said and rose from his chair and walked me outside to the car. It was a VW Polo, black and just over a year old. Daddy gave me the keys and told me that he could not have the boss of a new enterprise without her own transport. I was lost for words: I had learned to drive before going to college, but never had the need for a car as I always travelled on public transport.

The next day we all drove up to Oxford in my new means of transport, keeping to the back roads as much as possible. I parked in the car park and stood looking at the block of offices, which had been built in the Seventies with large windows and were beginning to look their age.

The letting agent took us into the entrance lobby, where there were two lifts and staircases going up on either side of them. We took the lift to the fourth floor and then walked down a long corridor, past several other offices which were occupied. The office we had come to see was at the far end of the corridor, and we entered a small reception area. A passage led off to two good-sized offices and a small kitchen area. There were two loos (which both looked as though they would need some attention) and a storage room about eight feet square.

After we had been shown round the office the agent left us to talk things over and said he would meet us downstairs.

Daddy looked at me. 'Do you think it will do?'

'It's bigger than I expected, and the rent on something this big may be more than we can afford.'

'You'll soon fill up the space, and the rents are within the budgets.'

Mum was standing by the window, and said, 'Come and look over here.' Pointing to some buildings away in the distance, she said, 'There could be your first customer, that's the John Radcliffe Hospital. And the Churchill Hospital is not far away. So tell Daddy yes, and perhaps he will sit still for a while next week.'

I said, 'Heaven knows when I shall ever be able to repay you, but yes, I think it will be fine.'

We drove back home and the rest of the weekend was spent around the dining room table, with lists of things to do and things that would be needed. I went back to West Manston Hospital with a thick folder of things that I still needed to know.

The head of our department had found a replacement for me, and asked me to show him the ropes. He said it should not be much trouble for him, as he had done it all before. That would leave me time to do a little research for my next big assignment. He was a colossal help in my last two weeks. The head of the department had managed to get me a letter of introduction to other hospitals and had spoken to the legal people and had a list of information that hospitals should legally be able to furnish me with. He winked and said, 'I see no reason why you can't start here.'

Next weekend when I returned home, we spent the time up to Sunday midday sorting out papers, with Mum putting them into folders and naming and numbering them. Then we drove back up to the office. When we reached the main entrance doors Daddy gave me the keys and told me to lead the way. When I opened the door into the reception area at first I thought we were in the wrong office. It had been painted out and had carpet tiles on the floor, and in the corner stood a small desk. Walking through, I found that everything had been painted and there were carpet tiles on all the floors. Both offices now were furnished with two desks each and chairs to match. Both now contained several filing cabinets, and there were more in the storeroom.

I looked at Daddy, who said, 'The workmen were here waiting to start at nine on Tuesday morning. And they only finished at eleven this morning. And after next week, we would never have managed to do it.'

Mum asked, 'What name will you put on the door? You have to call yourself something.'

I looked at Daddy in bewilderment. 'I have no idea. But Mum's right – we can't open an office in a week's time with no name for the company.'

Mum said, 'I think Medic Staff Agency seems to say it all, and that's my final choice.' And that's how the company name came into being.

* * *

The phone is ringing and I am not expecting a call. I pick up the receiver and hear Allen's voice at the other end.

'I hope you are ready for this. I've found a gym that does late sessions, and we are booked in for eight tonight, so get yourself ready. If we are going to do it, then let's start straight away; what do you think?'

My heart is pounding, but I say, 'That's fine with me. I'll be ready for half seven and look forward to seeing you then.'

'Good, I'll be there,' and the phone goes dead before I can change my mind. It all sounds so easy, but will I be able to walk out of the door when the time comes?

On Monday morning, after loading all the paperwork into the boot and back seat of my little car, Daddy and I set off for the office. I parked the car in our allotted space, and walked to the entrance door with arms full of folders. There, in shining new paint was the company name painted on the list of the companies occupying the building. When we reached the office, I read 'Medic Staff Agency' on a plaque fixed to the door.

It seemed to take forever to carry everything from the car up to the office and find a home for it all.

In the afternoon I said, 'I suppose we had better start on the real work.'

Daddy insisted that I have the larger of the two offices; he said, 'You'll soon need all the room you can find, and I'll be happier in the smaller one.'

During the afternoon I had several phone calls from friends to wish me well. The one that I appreciated most was from the West Manston Hospital with a few more contact leads to follow up. Daddy was on the Internet

45

and the phone, gathering more information and names to be contacted. We left the office at five-thirty and drove home tired but happy.

10

By the end of the week the mail was getting heavier, and it would be ten o'clock before it was all opened and put in order. And then the e-mails had to be checked and answered. The rest of my time was filled by feeding information into the computer. Daddy would help with this, but most of the time he kept himself to himself, and I could hear him on the phone or tapping away at his keyboard. By the end of the month I was having difficulty keeping up with all the things that needed to be done.

We advertised for a secretary in several publications. The answer that we both thought would fill the job was from a male nurse, and that's how I first met Allen. He started work two weeks later, and as soon as he had got used to us and could see exactly what we were intending to do, he just buried himself in the work and nothing was too much trouble for him. He lived not three miles from the office and would come into work on his bicycle unless it was raining. In time we were to become good friends but that was all, just good friends. He never offered any information on his life outside the office, and never asked about my private life, which suited me fine.

Three months after opening the office we not only had people on our books working for the NHS but also those in private practices, as well as in positions in care homes and in industry. It would be a long time before it was complete, but Daddy said we had enough to start advertising what we had. Then we could extend the service as and when we were ready. So we sent out booklets to all the hospitals that we had been in contact with, also to surgeries of general practitioners and those organizations working in the private sector. Daddy also posted our services on the Internet.

By the end of the following week several calls were coming into the office every hour, and thanks to the work that had been done over the last three months we were able to fill most of the requests we received. We were still receiving names to add to our lists, and it was becoming apparent that we would need another member of staff before long. With all the personal information on file I asked Daddy if we could increase the security of the office and the computer outlets. He told me that the computers were as secure as we could get them, and the following week a new door with special security locks was fitted to the entrance of the office

After that the workload increased and Linda Wordsmith joined the staff. She was in her mid-forties with hair that was already turning grey; she had been made redundant from her last position after twenty-two years of service. I took to her straight away, and she fitted in well – before long it seemed that she had always been there. Linda was given the task of dealing with the new people coming onto our lists and checking their credentials, Allen was dealing with the incoming requests for positions that needed to be filled, and the two of them worked together as though they had been doing it all their lives.

After six months we had an income enough to cover the staff wages and give me a little as well. I told Daddy it was time for him to give more of his time to Mum now that things had got off the ground. He was still coming to the office nearly every day, and although I knew I would miss him in the office I wanted him to enjoy his retirement. He said, 'I was thinking that you could manage things pretty much on your own now. And I would like some time away with Mum.'

Two weeks later they went off to the Caribbean on a three-week cruise. I went down to Southampton to see them off, and they waved to me from the upper deck as the boat left its moorings. When I returned home it felt strange to be walking about the house without them being there. I was now nearly twenty-five years old, and this was the first time I had ever been left at home on my own. And already I was looking forward to their homecoming.

Over the weeks Mum and Daddy were away we were all kept very busy. The phone never seemed to stop and the mail had grown, both incoming and outgoing. Allen and Linda were now in what had been my office and I had moved into what had been Daddy's office. They worked well together and I could hear them talking over problems as they arose. But it was now rare for them to bring the problems to me.

One of the difficulties we were finding was that now we were getting people from overseas wanting their names put on our register. The problem was that it was difficult to check their qualifications, and there was no way we could recommend them until we were satisfied that their CVs had been checked out to our satisfaction. One task I did take over in Daddy's absence was the accounts, and made sure that all the bills were out on time, and the incoming cheques were banked as they came in. I also opened another account into which I was determined to put something each month to help pay back all the expenses Daddy had shouldered since the beginning. It was only a few hundred to start with, but it would grow in time.

The week before Mum and Daddy were due back, I worked every evening in the garden so it would look nice for their return. On Saturday I made sure the house was clean and tidy, and the washing done and put away. They were due in at two o'clock on Sunday, and I made my way down to Southampton in Daddy's car in time to see the boat coming alongside. They both looked relaxed, happy and very tanned, and were so happy to see me. After loading their baggage in the back of the car I handed the keys to Daddy. He said, 'No thanks, we are on holiday until we reach home.' They sat in the back seat and held hands all the way.

During the next few months Daddy restricted his visits to the office to two or three days a week. But he was still interested in everything that was going on. He had also researched into the problem we were experiencing when checking on the credentials of people from overseas, and had made our job a lot easier.

Eventually I took one more person onto the staff, a young woman by the name of Ann, whose job it was to see to the incoming and outgoing mail, which took up most of her time. She also acted as receptionist and dealt with any callers and deliveries to the office. I was pleased because we were now self-sufficient, and paying the rent on the office, the insurance and other outgoings. The fund for the repayment of the money laid out by Daddy was also growing, though it would be a long time before I would be able to repay it all.

Daddy had been right when he told me to start with the most junior staff and work my way up, because in the end the more prominent people would follow. We were now getting requests for speakers to talk to students at seminars and other functions, and I advertised this fact in leaflets and on the Internet and invited those interested to contact the office. It was not long before we had added the names of several top surgeons and eminent specialists from gynaecology to brain surgery to our register.

After a year we had outgrown the space we had, and when the suite of offices became vacant next to mine I took it over so that the staff could be increased. The register now held 60 per cent of all those working in the public and private sectors of health care in England, and was still growing. Most important was that we held the names of over 75 per cent of those who were willing to stand in at short notice to cover the unexpected events in the working of the health care system – everything from a nurse needed to cover for a few days to top surgeons that might be needed at short notice to cover in case of unexpected emergencies.

Some alterations had to be done so that the extended office suite was still a self-contained unit and that the security was still as good as it could be made. When the new computers were installed I had a firm of computer specialists check over and update the security on the system we were using. As Daddy said, I did not only now run a company but was the owner of a very valuable asset. This was brought home to me when the government were debating the shortages of staff in the NHS and we were asked to identify areas that were most at risk. We had a minister come down to our offices to see how we had drawn our conclusions and why we had recommended certain actions. I smiled when he told me to send through the invoice for our expenses. When I told Daddy he said, 'If you start to work for the government without charging, they'll take up more of your time than you could afford.' So I duly sent in my account.

It was now getting near Christmas and I was looking forward to a few days at home with Mum and Daddy. Christmas had always been a special time at home for me, and this year I felt a break would do me a great deal of good. A week before Christmas, on a Friday I organized a night out for the staff, with dinner at one of the hotels in Oxford, and invited each to bring a partner or a friend with them.

Mum and Daddy were of course guests of honour, and I was proud to have them seated next to me. It was strange to see the members of staff in their finery and not in working dress, and it was good to meet the husbands and boyfriends of those you work with. Allen came with another man about his own age; he told me that they had met while they were at medical college and had kept in touch ever since. His name was Ben and had also left nursing because he had become a chronic asthmatic and could no longer fulfill the duties that the job required. After the meal Mum and Daddy went around the table and spoke to everyone there. By the end of the evening they probably knew more about the staff's partners than I did.

The trouble with short breaks is that they are over almost before they have begun: three days later I was back in the office, to be met with a backlog of enquiries. This would be the last time we ever closed the office over a holiday period; next time I would organize a skeleton staff to be on hand. because it would take us two days of hard work before things were back to normal. There were still other avenues to explore and expand, but I decided to put them on hold for a while and consolidate what we had.

The next April Daddy told me that he and Mum were planning to go on a trip to Australia and New Zealand and maybe Tasmania.

'We'll be away for at least a month; do you think you can manage on your own for that long?'

'I have promoted Allen to general supervisor, and he's now running much of the day-to-day workload, which leaves me to get on with the things I should be doing. Go and enjoy themselves and don't worry about me, I won't let anyone steal the shop while you're gone.'

They planned to leave the second week in May, and spent most of the time planning the route they would take. In the end they decided to fly to Sydney and stay there for a few days – a visit to the Opera House was a must – then travel up to Cooktown from where they could take in the Great Barrier Reef. Then to Alice Springs and see Ayers Rock, followed by a flight to Melbourne. The next destination was Tasmania, and from there on to New Zealand.

A week before they were due to leave I handed Daddy an envelope when he sat down to breakfast. He said, 'And what's all this? We don't usually communicate by the written word.'

'It's something for you and Mum, and you had better open it.' It was a cheque for ten thousand pounds as part payment for all the financial help they had given me. Both of them said that I should take it back because nobody knew what was around the corner, and I still might need it.

I said, 'The company is now on a sound footing, and this is something I want to do.'

When the day came for them to leave I took the morning off and drove them to Heathrow Airport to say goodbye and to remind them to keep me informed by postcard of their progress. They were so happy and I gave them both a hug before they vanished into the airport.

I had been thinking of extending our services into Wales and incorporating all the Welsh Hospitals and Health Trusts, and had prepared booklets to be sent to the relevant bodies. But I was still holding back because it would mean increasing the size of the office to accommodate the extra staff to deal with the project. As it was, everyone was always fully employed with a workload that was becoming larger rather than smaller. In the end I decided to leave it until Daddy returned and talk it through with him. They had been gone almost three weeks now, and I received a card from them almost every other day. It was a lot of travelling, but they were enjoying every minute of it.

Late one Thursday afternoon Allen and I were just finishing up before going home. I answered the knock on my door to two police officers, one male, the other female.

'Are you Jackie North?'

'Yes.'

'May we come in? Are you alone, or is anyone else in the office?'

I told them that Allen was in the other office but we were just on the point of going home. The woman called Allen in and he sat next to me. He asked, 'What's the trouble?'

She asked me, 'Do you know where your parents are at this time?'

'I'm not sure, they might be in Melbourne, Australia, or Tasmania.'

She then told me, 'Forty minutes into a flight that took off from Melbourne bound for Tasmania the plane vanished from the radar. Helicopters have flown over the route and wreckage has been found, but at this moment in time there are no signs of survivors. According to the flight records, your parents were on board.'

It was like a black curtain had been drawn over me. I sat there, too stunned to show any emotion. Allen held my hand, and I could hear him quietly sobbing.

I asked, 'When will you be certain there were no survivors?'

'After two hours the helicopters left the area; the sea is so deep at this point that it would be impossible to send divers down to check on the wreckage.'

I heard Allen say, 'She can't go home to a empty house,' then he went into the next office and I could hear him on the phone. When he came back he told them he had arranged for me to stay with someone for the night but he would stay until she arrived. Not long after that Linda arrived and the two officers left.

11

We left Allen to lock up and Linda drove me in silence to her house. When we got there she told me to go and shower and there would be pyjamas and dressing gown on the bed by the time I had finished. By the time I had showered and dressed, Linda had rung her doctor and explained what had happened. When I came downstairs he was sitting in the lounge with Linda. He was a man in his late forties with a strong but kind face, who asked, 'Do you mind my being here?'

I replied, 'I don't know what to think or what to do. I feel completely lost,' and then the floodgates opened and I wept as I had never wept before.

He sat in front of me and held both of my hands and talked to me in a soft voice. Eventually I got myself back under some sort of control. He gave Linda a sleeping draught to give me before I went to bed, and said he would call again tomorrow morning. He was one of the kindest men I have ever known.

Even with the sleeping draught I drifted in and out of sleep all night. And when eventually I got up, it was as though I was someone else. I knew there would be things to do, but my brain refused to tell me what they were. I must go home to put things in order, but the thought of going through the door and into an empty house frightened me. I would not be able to do it alone. Linda was sitting in the kitchen when I finally went downstairs. She had slept badly as well, and there were rings under her eyes.

She told me she had rung Allen and told him she would not be in today. He had said to take all the time I needed.

I asked Linda to come with me to my house. There would be things that I had to do, and people that would have to be seen. We sat and drank tea and I made lists of things to do and people to see. The doctor came back to see how I had slept, I told him that sleep would not come but I had dozed a little through the night. He asked if I would need another tablet for tonight, which I refused. He told me that if I needed him to give him a ring at any time, then left to continue his rounds.

I called Daddy's solicitor to tell him what had happened, and to ask his advice about what I should do now. And then the awful thought struck me that they were gone and I had nothing to bury; I began to cry again. He told me to meet him at his office on Monday morning, and he would see to everything for me. He would come to the house himself next week and we would be able to sort out things then.

In the afternoon we drove down to Wallingford, but before going to the house we went to the vicarage to see the vicar. We had never been regulars at church but had attended most church functions. He seemed genuinely upset at the news.

I said, 'As we can't hold a funeral I would like to have a memorial service. Daddy's solicitor will call on you to make the arrangements. Linda and I are going to see Mum and Daddy's friends; could you spare the time to come with us? I need moral support because none of them know about the crash yet. Some of them are getting old and I don't know how they will take it.'

He said, 'Of course I will, and if you like you can leave the talking to me. You are already distressed, and it might be easier coming from me.' For this I was eternally grateful, as it was a task I was dreading.

The round of calls we had to make took longer than I had expected, and without the vicar I would never had completed them. By the time we got back to the vicarage it was almost five. I thanked the vicar for his time and understanding and told him I would be in touch some time next week, then I drove to the house. I was glad Linda was with me, and when we reached the kitchen door I gave her the key and told her to open it. After punching the numbers into the alarm panel we walked in and I just stood there; I could not think of a single thing I needed to do.

Linda took my hand and said, 'Let's walk around the rooms, you have got to do it some time, and while you are with me it might as well be now.'

Everything was just as Mum and Daddy had left it; it still seemed as though they would walk in any moment. When we reached Daddy's study I opened his desk and started to cry again: there was the cheque I had given Daddy before they went away; he had never banked it. I put it in my bag and closed the desk again; the solicitor would have to sort out the rest of the papers in there.

I asked Linda, 'Is it all right for me to stay with you until Monday?'

'You can stay as long as you want to.'

We went back up to my bedroom and I showered and changed then packed a few things to take back to Linda's with me.

On Monday morning Linda said she should go back to the office – there would be nothing she could do if she was with me, and things would get behind if she did not go back to work. I waited until nine-thirty before ringing Daddy's solicitor, who must have been waiting for my call. He asked me to meet him at Wallingford at eleven, as the meeting would be better there than in his office.

I went down early and picked up milk and a few odd

things on the way. Going in this time was not as bad as the last time, until I noticed a pile of mail by the front door. One or two letters were for me, but most were for Daddy, and there in among the letters was a postcard from Mum. It must have been the last one she posted before leaving Australia for Tasmania. I sat alone in the hall and cried so hard I thought I would burst.

I had washed my face and tried to make myself look presentable before Daddy's solicitor arrived. His name was Mr Stroud, and he was in his late fifties, impeccably dressed in a dark suit, with grey hair. He came over as a man that you could talk to and he would listen. From the start he explained that what we had to talk about would be upsetting for me, but it had to be done.

'I've been in touch with the airline in Australia, and they have confirmed that your parents were definitely onboard the plane when it took off. The search has now been called off, and no bodies have been found.' He took an envelope from his briefcase and told me it was the last will that Mum and Daddy had made. They had drawn the document up in the solicitor's office, and Daddy had given it to him for safe keeping.

He asked, 'Have you touched or removed anything from the house since you first spoke to me?'

I took the cheque from my bag and handed it to him. 'I gave it to Daddy before he went away. He hadn't banked it, and I thought it foolish to leave it lying around. I don't quite know what to do with it now. The mail addressed to Daddy is on the desk for you to see and deal with.'

He looked at the cheque and a brief smile crossed his face. Picking up the letters he said, 'I can deal with them. The next question was, do you know anything about your father's financial affairs?'

'That was something that was never discussed. We lived well and never went without. Daddy had the proceeds from the sale of his import and export company, which were to fund his retirement. He helped me greatly whilst setting up my agency, and I was concerned it might eat into his retirement funds. That's why I tried to repay part of his expenditure.'

Mr Stroud said he would read me the will. It started with a few bequests to different charities, including five thousand pounds to our local church restoration fund. The rest of his estate, including the house and everything therein, any insurance that was due and moneys held in the bank or in shares or any other institutions, were bequeathed to his adopted daughter Jackie North. 'Mrs North's will reads exactly the same as Mr North's,' he added.

I said, 'I don't know if I can afford to stay on in the house on my own. I'll probably look for something smaller and easier to manage.'

He said, 'You have no idea how much you are now worth, do you?'

'Well no, I don't.'

'Without the house and all it contains, you are worth somewhere in the region of eight million pounds.'

The figure was so huge that it was impossible to take in. I said, 'I had no idea,' and he said, 'I know that, but it is true.'

He then asked me if I had opened the safe, which was behind a family portrait hung on the wall by the desk.

I said, 'I knew it was there, but I don't know how to open it.'

'I do, and with your permission I will do so.'

He removed some papers, which he put onto the desk, and then took out a small, very old leather-bound book that looked like a diary. This he placed in front of me and said, 'Can you remember seeing this before?'

'No ... but it looks familiar.'

'The last time you saw this was when you were five

years old; I was there at the time. This little book is not in your father's estate, because it is yours and there is a legal paper inside to prove it.'

I picked it up and opened it; it was a book filled with line drawings, and there on the front of the page was a name I could not believe. It read 'Vincent van Gogh', and as I turned the pages I could recall sitting on Daddy's knee with him turning the pages for me to look at the drawings.

Mr Stroud explained to me that he had no idea where my father had bought the little book, or how much he had paid for it. He thought Daddy had bought it at auction just before my fifth birthday, and he said he was pretty sure it was bought with me in mind. He asked me if I had any idea of its value, I said I had no idea – but it would never be sold while I was alive. Then I asked him if he would find out where it should be kept; the idea of leaving it where it was did not appeal to me at all. He said it would all be taken care of along with all the paper-work that would need seeing to.

After looking through the rest of the papers in the safe it was getting late. Mr Stroud said, 'Let's call it a day. I shall come back tomorrow and bring my secretary with me.' He started to put the things back in the safe, and then said, 'I think your mother's jewellery is still in the back of the safe,' and lifted out several boxes. One I recognized immediately: it was the box that contained the ring Daddy had bought her when they were in Holland. I opened the box and there it was. Poor Mum had only worn it once, and had not taken it with her when they went away on their last trip. I gave it back to the solicitor and he returned it to the safe.

When he had gone I rang Linda at the office and told her that I was going to stay at home tonight because the solicitor was coming back tomorrow, and I would need to be here. I asked her to tell Allen that I would be in the office on Wednesday and I would see her then. After thanking her for all the help and kindness she had given me over the last two days, I rang off. I was really tired and slept until seven next morning.

12

Looking from my window I can tell by the movement of the people walking along the pavement that it is getting late. I must shower and get myself ready for when Allen calls for me this evening. After all this time I still wonder if when the time comes I will be able to walk through the door. But it will be almost dark by then, and with Allen with me I am sure that it will be all right.

At twenty to eight Allen rings the bell of the front door. I push the button to let him in, and a few minutes later he knocks at the door of the apartment. I open the door to let him in but he says, 'Come on – I got held up and if we don't get a move on we'll be late.'

I grab my duffel and go to the door. 'Would you mind holding my hand until we get to the car?'

'Nothing will give me greater pleasure.' He grabs my hand and off we go.

On the short drive to the gym I wonder what on earth has kept me indoors for so long. All the little things that I had forgotten existed are suddenly remembered, and I have a job to stop myself from shouting out that I am on my way back.

Allen pulls up in front of the gym. 'Here we are then. The man in charge of this torture chamber is called Ted, and you'll need a microscope to find an ounce of fat on him. He's got a body like Charles Atlas.'

We walk in and are met by Ted, who is five feet eight

with not a hair on his shining head. His shoulders are broad and tapered down to his waist. His white sweatshirt is stretched across his chest and the muscles on his arms ripple as he moves. I can imagine him weightlifting when he has no customers, yet for such a powerful man his voice is gentle and I take to him straight away.

He has a clipboard in his hand and goes down a list of questions. I say, 'I haven't had any exercise for six months and am about sixteen pounds overweight.'

Allen says, 'I'm here because of Jack, and I need a very easy routine or I will probably die.'

After checking blood pressure and breathing Ted comes and holds his hand on the small of my back and tells me to bend down and try to touch my toes. 'OK, let's start with ten minutes on the bike, but take it easy. Then ten minutes on the rowing machine, and we will finish this session with ten minutes on the walker. That'll probably be as much as you will manage for a start.'

He is right: after half an hour I am bathed in sweat and ready for the shower. As we leave he gives us a few exercises to do at home, which will relieve the stiffness. We book to return the evening after next.

'That wasn't too bad, was it?' I say to Allen.

'You speak for yourself. If you are going to invite me in for coffee you will probably have to help me up the stairs and then back down again.'

On the drive back to the apartment I can't stop talking: I feel more alive than I have for months. When we get back Allen says, 'Well, do I get help up the stairs and a cup of coffee?' He climbs out of the car with a bundle of papers under his arm, and I grab his hand and pull him up the stairs.

He collapses into one of the chairs and I make the coffee. When we are both seated he hands me the papers he had brought. 'I think you ought to have a look at

64

these. This is something I have been working on for some time, and your opinion would be appreciated.'

I scan through what is being proposed. It's a novel idea I have never thought of. I can see problems from the start, but Allen has put a lot of effort into his investigations. Basically what he wants to do is to pull the expertise of the pharmaceutical development industry together, so that when new drugs are being developed the same experiments are not being duplicated in many different laboratories, thus saving hundreds, if not thousands, of hours of work for some of the cleverest people in the country.

I say, 'The industry and their shareholders will never allow it. This is one of the most secretive industries in the country, and their profits rely on that secrecy. And yet you think that they would allow us to hold the register of all the scientists and the things that they are working on?'

Allen puts his coffee cup on the table and looks at me. 'If I told you that the Department of Health has informed me that if it could be put into practice, they would be willing to help with the expenses of setting it up, would that change your mind?'

Allen is waiting for me to make a decision, one I cannot make until I have done some research for myself.

'All right, Allen; the idea is good and I shall have to give it a great deal of thought. If you get all your proposals and paperwork on my desk at the office for Monday morning, I shall be in and we can go through it all together. As from today I am out of hibernation. Thanks for your support tonight, and I would like you to come with me for the next couple of sessions, but right now I think sleep is the order for the day.'

I walk Allen to the door and kiss him on the cheek just before he leaves. He blushes and says, 'See you the day after tomorrow,' and is gone.

On my own again, the enormity of the decision to return to the office hits me, as from Monday I am determined that life will begin again. After putting the cups back into the kitchen I fall into bed.

At ten o'clock Mr Stroud and his secretary arrived with several fat folders which he laid out on the dining room table. He asked for permission to open the safe and said that he would call me if he needed anything else. I went out into the garden and spent most of the day there, cutting grass and pulling weeds. I went back in around three and he told me that he had almost done, but would I now stay while he went around the house to make a rough inventory of the furniture and effects.

It was almost six before he told the secretary to pack up the folders and put them in the car. He said it might be a week before he had anything more to tell me. I told him that I was going back to the office tomorrow so he could reach me there and asked him if he would see to the arrangements for the service for Mum and Daddy in the local church.

Next day I was in the office very early but found my desk clear of paperwork. I sat at the computer and looked back through the last few days' workload. I was just thinking that the company seemed to be running all right without me when Allen walked in. When I asked him how come my desk was clear, he said, 'I put in a couple of extra hours, that's all.'

Then he handed me the schedules for the day, pointing out that we had a doctor from America wanting to be placed on our register. 'He looks highly qualified but we are having difficulty checking him out; he won't answer e-mails, and he is never there when we have tried to phone him. I think you should deal with it.'

It was a normal busy day and it was three in the afternoon before I got round to the American doctor. Putting through a phone call to the number we had been given, a woman answered. She said he was out at the moment and she was not sure when he would be back. I tried to get another number to call, but was told she never had one. After putting down the phone I sat thinking that something did not sound quite right. I decided to go to the top and made a call through to the FBI

After being put through several different departments I heard a woman's voice. I explained the problem we were having, but he seemed to have the qualifications we were looking for and we did not want to lose him. After taking all the details she asked me to hold. It was not long before she was back on the line.

'It's no wonder you couldn't get hold of him – he's still in prison. He tricked his way into a position in a hospital with false qualifications. While working in an accident and emergency department he killed a young girl in a bungled attempt to stop internal bleeding. He's due to be released in two weeks' time after serving six years.' She asked if I wanted to bring any charges against him. I said, 'Yes, he should stay in prison for the rest of his life.'

I told Allen what I had found out and how lucky for us that we were so thorough with our checks. This was just the type of person that could slip through. I held a short staff meeting and told them as well, saying that if there was any doubt at all to refer it to either Allen or myself. 'It's better to lose one or two than let a rogue one get through.'

When the staff had left I told Allen how grateful I was for all he had done in my absence, and that I thought that we could do with one more staff. Everyone was working as hard as they could and we had no spare person for when anyone was away. As from now he was in overall charge of the day-to-day running of the office, answerable only to me, and his pay was increased to reflect the added responsibility. I asked if he would like Linda as his assistant; she seemed able to communicate with the rest of the staff in a easy manner and was good at her job. Allen looked a little embarrassed but thanked me and said he would always do his best.

It was well over a week before Mr Stroud rang me to make a date for another meeting at his office. When we met he took me into an office that seemed to be almost full to bursting point: books and papers bundled up with coloured string were piled against every wall. He sat behind his desk and I sat on the other side. He opened a folder and looked at me for some time.

'When we first met at the house I gave you a estimate of the value of your father's assets, and how much you would be likely to receive. Now that I have had time to go into all of his assets, I find the figure is not eight million pounds, it is eleven million. Plus the house, which is valued at six hundred thousand; and the furniture, some of which are good antiques, could raise a further three hundred thousand. Your mother's jewellery, including the ring your father bought her in Holland, looks like another one hundred thousand. So it looks like the total will be around twelve million pounds. But you must remember that the Government is going to take a large slice of that before you get it. Is there anything else I can do, and are there any questions you wish to ask?'

'The house has been my home for many years, but is far too big for me to look after – if I stay there I will only use one room. I will look for an apartment in Oxford, which will be easier to look after, and I'll be nearer the office. It would be nice to furnish the apartment with furniture from home, then dispose of what I do not need.'

Mr Stroud thought for a few moments then asked if I had the funds to purchase a property of my own or would I need an advance. 'You see, it will still be a few weeks before I can transfer the capital over into your name. But we should be able to advance you five hundred thousand pounds; you must say if that is not enough.'

'A fortnight ago I thought ten thousand was a lot of money, and I'm sure that the amount you suggest will be more than enough to cover everything.'

He asked, 'What will you do when it is all sorted out, and what do you intend to do with the book of drawings? The interest from the money will amount to several thousand pounds a week, and the need to earn a living by running the office will no longer be necessary.'

'I need to finish what's been started, and my working life won't change in the foreseeable future. As for my little book of drawings, would you contact the museum in Amsterdam to see if they would like to have it on loan? It seems a pity to have it locked in a vault when it could give so much pleasure to people in the real world.'

He replied that in a few days everything I had asked would have been seen to and he would give me another call to finalize the details. Before I left he told me that he had arranged for a remembrance service in the church in Wallingford for a week on Saturday. Handing me a list of people he thought I might wish to invite, he said he would be glad to see to the invitations to people who had worked with and for Daddy. I thanked him for his kindness and left.

It was past midday and I had not eaten breakfast, so I had a light lunch in town before going back to the office. I must have looked pale because Allen asked if I was all right, and he could manage if I wanted to have the rest of the day off. I said I would stay but would work on private matters, and sat down at my desk. For the rest of the day I wrote out the invitations to attend the memorial service from the list given me by Mr Stroud. These I gave to Ann and asked her to see that they went with the next post.

When the staff left at the end of the day I asked Allen and Linda to stay for a while. I told them that when the will was published they were bound to find out that I was now a very wealthy woman. But as far as I was concerned it was going to be work as usual. What we were doing needed to be done, and I was determined to do the job properly. I then asked Linda if it was all right for me to stay the night at her house, as I could not face going home to an empty house tonight.

At Linda's home we prepared a meal and whilst we ate I told her that I had decided to sell the house and buy an apartment in Oxford. I told her that I did not know the first thing about buying property but next week if she would accompany me, we could call on a few estate agents. I told her a little about the money but not the amount. I began to cry and told her I would burn the lot just to have them back with me again.

Before we went to bed I asked if she would accompany me to the church service. She said, 'You try and stop me! As a matter of fact all the staff that can be spared at work want to be there but some will have to stay to look after things at the office.'

The next week was hectic and I found little time for the office. I had sent out the invitations to friends of the family and called to see the vicar. I chose the hymns for the service and arranged for the church to be bedecked with flowers. In the evenings the phone never stopped, with people ringing to say that they would attend and offering their condolences.

On the Friday night I drove up to Oxford and picked up Linda, who had offered to stay with me for the night and accompany me to church next day. When we returned I had calls from Allen to say he would see me tomorrow, and then from Mr Stroud to make sure that all was well.

As arranged with the vicar Linda and I arrived early, and the vicar showed us to our seats. I had already told him that Allen and Mr Stroud were to sit with me in the front pew. He introduced three members of the church who were to act as ushers and to seat everyone. Allen and the rest of my staff were the first to arrive, and I directed Allen to sit with me and the rest to take the pew behind me. The church began to fill, and before the service started people were standing at the back and along the walls at the side. Just as the vicar came in Mr Stroud appeared and sat next to Allen. He looked at me and said in a low voice, 'I think they have all managed to get in.'

The service went well: the vicar spoke highly of both Mum and Daddy, and the congregation sang the hymns with gusto. When it was all over Mr Stroud, Allen and Linda and the vicar walked me to the entrance door of the church. As the congregation came out I shook them by the hand, thanking them for coming. Most spoke of their sorrow and said they would think of me in the coming weeks and months and wished me well.

It was nearly an hour before the last of them left the church, so I invited Mr Stroud, Linda, Allen and the vicar back to the house for a drink. We sat in the kitchen and I made tea and put out some sandwiches that Linda had made earlier. Allen went into the dining room and came back with a glass of brandy and told me to drink it. Spirits are something I usually do not touch, but as the drink went down it seemed to relieve the emptiness that was gnawing away at my inside.

We chatted for a while and then the vicar said he must get back to get ready for the evening service. I told him to hold on for just a minute and went into Daddy's study and brought back an envelope and handed it to him.

'What is this?' he asked.

'Open it and see.' It was a cheque for ten thousand pounds made out to the church restoration fund; I had rewritten the cheque that had been given to Daddy. The only thing I asked was that a small memorial plaque to Mum and Daddy be put somewhere in the church.

When he saw what it was his eyes opened wide, but all he said was, 'Thank you,' and put the cheque in his pocket and he said he would see to it. After he had gone I managed to get Mr Stroud on his own and told him what I had done. He said my parents would have liked that and that he approved of my actions. Soon after that he and Allen left to drive back to Oxford, leaving Linda and me to sit and talk until bedtime.

13

On Monday and Tuesday morning Linda and I went around estate agents picking up pamphlets for apartments in and around Oxford. I found two that looked promising and made arrangements to view both on Friday afternoon. On Wednesday I was in the office all day and asked Allen to come and see me. I told him that we must get on with the move to take Welsh hospital and health personnel on to our register, because before the end of the year I was determined to include those in Scotland as well.

Allen said he had heard that another suite of offices was about to become vacant in our block, and it might be prudent to acquire them before anyone else stepped in. I was pleased he was thinking on the right lines and told him to make all the arrangements, and I would pass them to my solicitor.

On Friday afternoon I met the estate agent and went to view the apartments. The first was not bad but did not live up to its description. The second was nearer to the city centre and on the third floor, but it was perfect, and I said I would take it. It still had ninety-five years of a ninety-nine-year lease to run, and the price was not exorbitant. I asked when I could take possession, but that I did not want it to be longer than a month. The agent told me that if the solicitors could agree he could see no problem and that I should get my solicitor on the case as soon as possible.

This I did and then went home and listed all the things

that I would need to take with me to furnish what was to be my new home. I told Mr Stroud that when the conveyance went through and I had moved what I required, I wanted him to see to the disposal of the remaining furniture and the house. When I moved into the apartment I did not wish to return to the house again; it would be very distressing to return and find it empty.

It was exactly four weeks before I had the key, and a week later I moved in. It was everything I needed with plenty of room, good security and a view from the window down a quiet street.

Over the next ten weeks we increased the staff by two and moved into the other office. Our enterprise now occupied most of the top floor of the building. But most important was the fact that now we were well on the way to 70 per cent of the Welsh workforce included on our register, and enquiries were beginning to come in.

Our register was now the most comprehensive of its kind in the country. We were getting enquiries from government departments almost every week. Although they always paid the account at the end of each month, this began to concern me. I wrote to the Minister of Health, explaining who we were and the service we provided, and asked if he could find the time to see me. I was surprised when I received an invitation to meet the Minister at the House of Commons on the following Thursday.

The meeting was for eleven and I was in good time. Someone came to fetch me and lead me to a much smaller office than I was expecting. The Minister was sat at a desk and asked me to be seated, and then asked how he could be of assistance. I explained who I was and what my company did, to which he said that he already knew this, and what were my concerns.

I said, 'We are receiving quite a number of enquiries from your department, things that the department should already know. It is my concern that the government is testing us to see if we are holding too much information on too many professional people in the health service, because we also deal with the private sector as well, and the great majority of those are also on our register. We do not want to run foul of anyone, especially the government.'

'I am sorry that you have come to this conclusion. The department has been keeping a eye on your company for some time, and has come to the conclusion that the information held by you is far ahead of that held by us. The department is grateful for the information that we have received from you, and enquiries will continue to be made.'

I told him, 'We have just moved into the health providers in Wales, but are only at about seventy per cent of the workforce.'

He said, 'The department knows about this, but you have done well in about ten weeks.' I had not realized just how close an eye they had kept on us, and vowed to keep a closer check on our security. I thanked him for meeting me, and as I left he said that no doubt we would be hearing from his staff again in the near future.

As always when we extended the area that we covered, the workload seemed to double because of all the checks that had to be made on all the personnel before entering them on to our register and providing all the potential clients with every aspect of our services, not to mention advertising in the medical journals for anyone with the appropriate medical qualifications to come forward to have their names added to our register. It was two hard months before I was happy that the move into Wales was going well.

The following week there was a good show on at the Oxford Theatre so I asked Linda and Allen if they would like to come with me to see it and bring a friend if they wished. Linda said she would be fine and Allen asked if he could bring Ben, the chap who had accompanied him to the Christmas party. I said that was fine with me and I would try to get tickets for Friday night.

I managed to get four tickets in the second row of the stalls, and arranged to meet up with them outside the theatre just before seven-thirty. I drove to a small car park not far from the theatre, and when I arrived the other three were already there. It was not until then that I realized that I had left my evening bag in the car, and the tickets were in it. Linda said she would come with me but I said, 'No, it won't take a minute,' and hurried off to where I had parked the car.

14

As I was reaching in to get the bag a large old and very dirty white van pulled into the space beside me. I heard the side door open and then someone grabbed me from the back, at the same time clamping a hand over my mouth. The next minute I was pulled through the side door and into the back of the van, and I heard the door slide shut. The man who was holding me was large and powerful and I could not get away from him. I could hear him shouting to the driver, 'Go, go, go,' and then the van was moving.

He wrapped a blindfold around my head and said, 'If you start to scream I'll break your neck.' Then he shouted to the driver, 'You know where to go, so get on with it.'

I thought, 'My God, I'm being kidnapped. They must know who I am, and have found out that I am worth a great deal of money.'

I was terrified and asked the one holding me what it was he wanted. He just laughed and said, 'I want everything, and I'll make sure I get it before the end of the night.'

The van must have been driving down a very straight road because I had not felt it turn for a long time. When it did turn off it turned to the left and continued for a short time and then we were on an unmade road and the van bumped over ruts until it came to a stop. After the driver had stopped the engine the man holding me told him to get out and make sure that nobody came.

Now he said to me, 'You can enjoy the next half hour or make it hard for yourself.'

It suddenly dawned on me that I had not been kidnapped for ransom; this animal intended to rape me. I began to struggle but it was useless; he was much too powerful and began to rip my dress from my body. Soon I realized that I must be almost naked and he was trying to climb on top of me. I brought up my knee and hoped that it would hit him in the groin, but I must have missed. The next thing I felt was a terrific blow to the side of my head and a blinding flash of light, then I must have passed out.

When I came round I was shivering, and although my head was bursting I could see the moon and the stars in the sky. I was laid on the grass by the side of a track that led to an open barn, and what was left of my clothes was thrown down beside me. When I sat up I could see in the distance the cooling towers of Didcot Power Station – the van and those in it were gone.

I dressed myself the best I could, but my dress was in ribbons and I could only wrap it around myself and hold it to stop it falling off. My head hurt and I felt dizzy when I tried to stand, and the vision in my left eye was blurred. Slowly I made my way down the rutted track and eventually came to a proper road. I could see the lights of a village but they were a long way off. I was not sure that I would be able to walk that far, but there was nothing in the other direction so I began to walk towards the lights.

After I had been walking for what seemed to be a long time, a car came up behind me. I turned and waved for it to stop and my dress that I had been holding up almost fell to the ground. The car stopped and a man got out and asked if I needed assistance. I can remember saying, 'Thank God,' and then I must have passed out again.

This time when I came round I was in the back of the car with a woman holding me. When they realized I was back with them the man asked what had happened to me. His wife said, 'Never mind about that – drive her to a hospital and make it quick.'

Before he started the car my head had cleared a little and I was thinking again; I asked whether they had a mobile phone. His wife said yes, so I asked if they would phone the police and wait with me here until they came – it was important that I take them to the place were it happened and the sooner the better. He made the call and was told to stay where we were and a patrol car would be with us in fifteen minutes. He then got out of the car and went to the boot, came back with a huge blanket and his wife wrapped it round me.

The lady said they were Mr and Mrs Wise; they lived in Didcot and were just on their way home. I said, 'It looks as though it will be some time before you get there, as the police will want to talk to you before you leave.' She said, 'Never mind that; you should be at a hospital. You have a terrible lump and bruise on the side of your face.' I felt better just sitting next to her; she was in her sixties and reminded me of Mum.

It was not long before the police car arrived. There were a male and female officer, who asked me to come to the car and explain what had happened to me. I asked them if Mrs Wise could come with me because I would feel more comfortable if she were there. They looked at each other and agreed, and asked Mr Wise to wait in his car.

I sat in the back of the police car with Mrs Wise, who held my hand. The two officers were in the front and I started to tell them what had happened, from the time the man had grabbed me while I was at my car in Oxford. I continued, trying not to leave anything out up to the time I found myself on the grass by the track leading to the open barn, then the walk until Mr and Mrs Wise stopped to see what was matter the with me.

By the time I had finished another police car had arrived and pulled up behind us. The woman officer asked whether I felt up to showing them the track leading to the barn, or did I wish to be taken to the hospital. I told them I would show them, and Mrs Wise said she was coming with me. One of the officers went to see Mr Wise and the officers in the other car. Then we went in convoy back to where the rough track met the road.

The open barn could be seen in the pale moonlight; it was about three hundred yards from where we had stopped. I told the police that when I had regained consciousness I was lying on the grass on the left-hand side of the track just before the barn. It would appear I had been pushed out of the side door, the same one the man had pulled me through in the first place, then what was left of my clothes had been thrown out after me.

The police did not want to go down the track in the darkness, as there was a good chance of disturbing evidence that might be visible in daylight. One of the police cars and its crew stayed at the entrance to the track. The other one took me and Mrs Wise to the hospital in Oxford, with Mr Wise following behind. I asked the officers to contact Allen and Linda and tell them that I had been found. They must have be worried to death because a long time had elapsed since I had left them at the theatre to retrieve the tickets from my car.

At the hospital I was put into a room on my own; Mrs Wise stayed with me until the doctor arrived with a nurse to examine me. He asked, 'What happened to you? Do you think you were raped?'

I told him that I had been unconscious from the time I had been hit on the side of the head, but I was certain that the men had raped me. He examined the swelling on the side of my face and said, 'You've been hit with great force, but it doesn't look as though anything is broken. In the morning you're going to have a very black eye, and it's going to be sore for a few days.'

The doctor then asked if he could examine the rest of my body, and he and the nurse gently removed my clothes. These were deposited in a plastic bag and then, tying the top, the nurse placed it on a table at the side of the room.

The examination was gentle but thorough; he asked about some bruises on my breasts. I said that they were not there before, the doctor said they looked like bite marks and continued to write things down on his pad. When he had finished he confirmed that I had indeed been raped. He said that it looked as though the man had used a condom because they had detected no semen. The nurse had taken swabs from my breasts, then told me that there was a good chance that tests would discover saliva, and that would provide a DNA sample.

I was then given a hospital gown and taken to a private room and put into bed. The doctor said he would look in on me later and said there was a Detective Sergeant Holt outside the door who wanted to talk to me. He went to the door and I heard him talking to the detective; I could hear a woman's voice as well. When Detective Sergeant Holt came into the room he was accompanied by a female officer, who asked me if I felt well enough to answer a few questions.

I said, 'I'll do my best, but I told the other officers everything I can remember.'

The detective pulled a chair over to the side of the bed and the female officer stood behind him. He opened a small book and began to ask questions. He must have talked at some length to the other officers, because he knew everything that I had told them. He asked, 'Do you know the make of the van?'

'I only glanced at it as it pulled up beside me. I was leaning into my car to reach my bag, which was on the passenger seat. I only saw it out of the corner of my eye, but it was very dirty.'

'Was there anything in the back of the van?'

'Before I was blindfolded I saw what looked like bales of rags or cloth. And the man sat on these while holding me while the van was driven away.'

'Did you see the man at all?'

'He held me from the back all of the time, so I never got a look at him. But he was a large man and very powerful; once he held me, there was nothing I could do.'

He said, 'What about the driver?'

'I only saw the back of his head. I would say he was the smaller of the two and he had a full head of dark, if not black wavy hair.'

'Now was there anything special about his voice?'

'The man who grabbed me sounded as though he was a local man, but the driver didn't speak at all.'

When he had finished he thanked me for all my help and said he would keep me informed of progress. He said that they were taking my clothes with them, and they would be sent to Forensics for testing. He also asked if the doctor had asked me for a DNA sample, I told him that he had and I had let him take it.

I asked, 'Have Allen and Linda been contacted?'

The female officer said, 'They are in the waiting room. Mrs Wise is also still here and would like to say goodbye before she and her husband leave.'

I asked the detective if he would send Mrs Wise in first. She came and sat by the bed and wanted to know how I was feeling now. I told her the doctor had given me something to calm me down, and I felt better now I was warm in bed. She told me to keep in touch, and that she and her husband would be thinking of me. Then she left, telling me to get plenty of rest.

When Linda and Allen came in I could see that Linda had been crying, and when she saw me she started again. She said, 'It's all my fault – if I had walked with you back to the car it would never have happened.'

I said, 'It's not anybody's fault, especially not yours; it was the animals that roamed the streets that were to blame.'

Allen was looking at my face and wanted to know if the doctors were doing anything to help with the swelling and the blackness around my eye. He looked close to tears as well; none of us knew what to say. I told him the doctor had given me something for the pain and it was beginning to make me feel sleepy. They said their goodbyes and I drifted into an uneasy sleep.

The doctor and a nurse came to see me early the next morning. He checked me over and gently felt the side of my face. He assured me that nothing was broken and said they had run tests on the samples taken the night before and they had all proved clear. He said that he had contacted a counsellor and arranged for her to come and see me later that morning, and that the Detective Sergeant wanted to talk to me again this afternoon.

I asked if I could have a shower, but the doctor said he would rather I let a nurse wash me, and maybe tomorrow I could shower. After they had left I lay there, trying to remember every little detail of what had happened. When the nurse came to wash me I had not remembered anything I had not already told the police. She was about thirty and a bit overweight, but she had gentle hands. As she was washing round the back of my neck, she asked how I came by the red line just above my shoulders. I said I had no idea, then it all came back: I had been wearing the gold and diamond cross Daddy had given me on his return from Holland, and now it was gone. The chain must have been broken when my dress was ripped off.

Next was the counsellor. She seemed young for the job she was doing, but was pleasant to talk to. We talked for over an hour, and she seemed in no hurry to leave. She wanted to know about my life and the work that I did. She only touched on what had happened last night and appeared to be more concerned about my face than anything else. She said that I would be in hospital for about two more days and asked if I would like her to call again. I told her that if she had time I would be glad to see her tomorrow, if she could fit me in.

They brought me lunch but the tray went back almost untouched; the coffee was welcome, and the nurse brought me another cup a little later on. The detective and his companion came back at four and had a few more questions to ask. I told him that I had been wearing the gold and diamond cross and now it was gone, and showed him the mark on my neck where the chain had been broken. He asked me to describe it in detail, and I sketched it in his notebook. He wanted to know the value of the cross; I told him it was a present from Daddy and I did not know how much it had cost. It was bought from a diamond merchant in Holland and I thought it probably had been expensive. He said the police would circulate the description of the cross and see if it turned up anywhere. He told me that things were moving along; they now had quite a few leads to follow up, and he would be back tomorrow if there was anything more he wanted to know.

Linda came in the evening and brought me some new underwear, as well as slacks, sweater and shoes.

I said, 'If all is well in the morning I can go back to my apartment in the afternoon.'

She told me, 'Give me a ring when you know, and I'll get a taxi and come to collect you. Would you rather come and stay at my house for a day or two before going back?'

'I'd like to go to the apartment, but if you would stay with me there for the first night I would be grateful.'

'I'll throw some night things in a bag when I get back home. Allen wanted to come with me tonight, but he thought it best to wait until you were out of hospital. He also told me not to stay too long, and that rest was the best thing for you at the moment.' Soon after that she left, and I listened to the radio until I fell asleep.

The following morning the doctor came to see me again and told me that I could go home after his afternoon rounds. He said that Detective Sergeant Holt was in the waiting room and wanted to see me again.

The detective had the female officer with him and sat in the chair beside the bed. He said, 'We have arrested a man in connection with your kidnap and the following rape. Pictures from a security camera in the car park show a white van pull up beside you and your car. Moments later it drives away and you are no longer there. One of my officers recognized the van as belonging to a man we have had under surveillance for some time. When our officers confronted him he admitted driving the van but says he did not touch you. We have the name of the other man and hope to pick him up today. You will be pleased to know we found your gold and diamond cross in the back of the van, and the broken chain. But we must keep it until after these people have been to trial.'

The counsellor came to see me later and we talked for an hour. This time I found that it was I who did most of the talking; she just listened. She gave me her telephone number and said, 'Ring me anytime. It won't matter if it's in the dead of night, you will still reach me. And you will be amazed how talking or shouting at someone will help.'

The police had allowed Allen to take my car back to my parking lot at the apartment; my bag and keys were still with the car, and he had given them to Linda. When the taxi picked me up from the hospital we went straight to the apartment. Once there I poured two glasses of brandy and ran a deep hot bath. Lying in the bath sipping the brandy I talked to Linda through the open bathroom door. I told her that the police had been to the hospital and had photographed the injuries to my face, and I had signed a statement that had been prepared. I had brought a copy of it home with me.

When Linda had left to go to the office the next day, I waited a while and then rang Mr Stroud. I explained the bare facts to him over the phone and asked if he would come to see me at his earliest convenience. He sounded shocked and said, 'I'll be round straight away; would it be all right if I brought my secretary with me – I want a record of the meeting.' I thanked him and replaced the receiver, it was then that I started to shake. I did not feel cold but could not stop shaking, I suppose because of the shock of what had happened setting in.

When he arrived I asked his secretary if she would make us all a cup of tea and to make mine sweet. I was still shaking and sat with a thick blanket wrapped round me. She looked at my damaged face and asked if she should call my doctor. I said that I would be all right after a cup of tea and she went off to the kitchen. I handed Mr Stroud the copy of the statement I had signed for the police at the hospital, and he read through it twice.

He asked, 'Have you remembered anything else since you made the statement?'

I told him it was as comprehensive as I could make it – I had been over the night's events time and time again, and there was nothing to add.

He brought a paper out of his briefcase (the one Daddy had always carried, which I had given to him) and asked me to sign at the bottom. This was to show that I had authorized him to act on my behalf; it would be needed when he called at the police station later that day.

Mr Stroud said, 'I won't handle the case when it finally comes to court; that will be the job of a criminal lawyer or even a barrister. But if you are happy to let me see to things, I shall make sure you have the best there is.' They stayed and talked for about an hour, then he said he had to go to the police station and start the ball rolling. He wanted to let his secretary stay with me and pick her up when he had finished at the station, but I assured him that I would be all right.

Allen rang me during the day and came to see me in the evening. He brought with him two national newspapers. Both had the story of 'Wealthy Oxford businesswoman kidnapped and raped. Left naked in open countryside. Two men being held in connection with the attack.' Both papers covered the story in detail, but I did not read it all.

When I put the papers down, Allen said, 'Reporters have already tried to talk to Linda and me. We brushed them off and told them we had nothing to say. You must expect them to turn up here sooner or later; it might be a good idea to vanish for a few days. If you stay, it would be as well not to answer the phone because they are persistent.'

Allen was embarrassed to talk about what had happened; instead he suggested that I stay away from the office until the marks on my face had healed and the reporters had found somebody else to chase. 'Linda can manage as long as you phone in once a day to deal with any problems that may arise.' As we talked the phone started to ring. Allen asked, 'Are you expecting a call?'

'No, unless it's Linda.'

He picked it up and I heard him say, 'She's not here.' Then a little while later he said, 'She's gone away, and I don't know when she will return, but it will not be until after people like you have stopped chasing her,' and he slammed down the phone.

There were very few people who knew my mobile number, so I told Allen to ring me on that and to give it to Linda. I would ring Mr Stroud and the police, and tell them to only use that number. The house phone could then be unplugged. Allen said that should be all right, as long as I did not answer the door or go out. We left it at that and Allen said, 'I'll call again tomorrow and give you a ring first thing in the morning.'

At nine next morning I rang the police to tell them that if they needed to contact me to only ring me on my mobile number and to give it to no one else – especially not to reporters or any members of the press.

Next I rang Mr Stroud and told him the same thing. He apologized and said, 'I should have thought of the press and should have warned you. I have been to the police and they have co-operated in every way. I've also been in touch with a criminal lawyer, who is now looking at all the evidence which has been gathered so far. The police have arrested both of the men concerned, and they will be before the Magistrates Court to be charged tomorrow. The lawyer will be there and assures me that they will not get bail. He will want to see you, but I shall be there. Don't worry about anything, and get well again.'

15

That evening Allen came just after seven with a bottle of wine and some nibbles. He also had a bundle of mail in his hand. First I skipped through the letters; they were all handwritten, but I did not recognize any of the writing. Most were from Mum and Daddy's friends who had been at the church service. All were supportive, and it pleased me that everyone had taken the time and trouble to write them.

Two were from women who had gone through similar experiences as myself, and they urged me to get the best possible lawyer to represent me. Both said that the defence lawyer they had to face had tried to make it look as though they were to blame for what happened to them. In both cases the defendant had gone to prison, but with remission the longest either of them would serve would be three and half years. One of the women said that when the man concerned got out she was going to kill him, and asked me to destroy the letter when I had read it.

For the remainder of the evening Allen talked about the office. He said there had been a few reporters on the phone, and one had even come to the office and asked to see me. They had all been told the same story, that I had gone away for a time and had not left a contact number. He said he would call again tomorrow evening. I gave him a list of things I needed, and if there were any more letters sent to the office to bring them too.

When he had gone I reread the two letters from the women who had written about their experiences in court, and then hid them in my desk.

The following afternoon Mr Stroud brought the criminal lawyer to see me. He was in his late thirties, with dark hair that was already beginning to show signs of going grey. He stood very erect and looked comfortable in his dark suit. He removed a hefty pile of paper from his briefcase, and laid it on the table beside him.

'This is what we have so far; it is the statement you gave to the police in hospital and the photographs that were taken of your injuries. We have the statements of both of the men who have been charged, and the charges that have been brought against them, which are kidnap, physical assault and rape. They have been remanded in custody until the trial, which should be in about four to six weeks' time and will take place at the Crown Court here in Oxford.'

He then went through my statement line by line, putting different emphasis on different words; some of the time the way he read things put a different meaning on the words than the one which I had intended. He made copious notes all the time we were talking, going back over some points several times. When we got to the end of the statement he asked if there were witnesses present when I signed it. I told him that Detective Sergeant Holt had been there, and also the woman officer who had accompanied him every time he had come to see me.

The lawyer then read the statement of the man who said he had been the driver of the van. 'He said that he had pulled up beside your car, you were half-in half-out of the car at the time. His mate had opened the side door and started talking to you. He said that you had voluntarily got into the van and his mate had told him to drive away. He had driven to a quiet place over near

Didcot and got out of the van and went for a walk. When he returned his mate had turned the van around and was in the driver's seat. He had asked where the woman was and had been told that you had taken fright and run away. They then drove back to Oxford and went for a drink.'

He then said that the next statement, given by the man in the back of the van, was even worse, and I should not say anything until I had heard that as well. This statement stated that I had agreed to go with him and I had said that I fancied him and got into the van without even being asked. We had petted right up to the time the driver had got out. But when things got serious I had told him I would not do it. 'He stated that you had a bit of a fight and in the end he had pushed you out of the van but had never raped you. When his mate returned they drove back to Oxford and went for a drink.'

I was stunned, and the lawyer asked if I was all right. I said, 'That was a pack of lies from start to finish. You only have to look at the report of the hospital, and what about the evidence from the security camera. Ask Mr and Mrs Wise, they will tell you the state I was in when they found me. I don't think that I looked as though I had been in a bit of a fight – I had been knocked unconscious and could hardly see out of my left eye.'

He said, 'They only have your word as to what happened at the van. And although the van had been seen on the camera, it did not show the side with the door. That part of what happened could not be stated as fact. It is just your word against theirs.'

'What about the rape?' I asked.

'With the evidence of the doctors that will not be hard to prove, but I must warn you this will not be a nice, clean-cut case.'

I then asked if he knew the name of the person who

would be handling the defence. He said it was a lawyer named Madden, who had a reputation for bending the rules. My thoughts went to the two letters in my desk; I was sure that he had been mentioned in one of them, but I thought it best not to mention them to the lawyer at this time.

Allen and Linda were coming to see me most days, and my face was now beginning to look a little bit more normal. I had been cooped up in the apartment for two weeks and wanted to get back to work. Mr Stroud and the lawyer had been to see me on two more occasions, and I asked if they thought I should go back to the office. They both agreed that it was far better if I waited until after the trial. The lawyer said he was taking advice from a barrister who wanted to see me, but it would be in his office and he would accompany me.

The meeting with the barrister consisted of the same questions all over again. He asked, 'How do you feel about the trial?'

'I don't understand your question. But if you mean do I want to see the men who did this to me in jail, then the answer is yes.'

'It won't be a pleasant experience for you, but if you want to proceed with the case against them, I will be happy to assist. The start of the trial is in ten days' time, and I shall see you at the court before it gets under way.'

In the days leading up to the trial Mr Stroud and the lawyer came to see me four more times, each time to verify different parts of the statements. Their last call was two days before the trial, and I produced the two letters I had been sent by the other victims of rape. I drew the attention of the lawyer to the name of the man in charge of the defence in one of the cases.

I said, 'It appears that I'm going to be his next victim, unless you can prevent him.'

'Can I take the letter with me?'

'You can make a copy of it but not the last remarks; those are private between me had the writer.'

He made the copy in longhand, omitting the last part, and put it in his briefcase. 'I'll pass the information on to the barrister as soon as I return to my office.'

16

At last the day of the start of the trial came, and I was collected from the apartment by Mr Stroud. He said, 'I think you should be warned; there will be a lot of people waiting outside the court. And as soon as we get there I will see that you are escorted in as soon as possible.'

He was right – when the car came to a stop it was surrounded by news cameramen and reporters. The police cleared a way for us to enter the courthouse building. All the time questions were being shouted at me and cameras and mikes were pushed toward my face. As instructed by Mr Stroud, I kept quiet.

We entered the court and I could see my lawyer seated with the barrister at a table at the front. Mr Stroud escorted me to them and then took a seat just behind them. They told me not to be afraid of the surroundings and just remember what I had been told. Soon after that the jury was brought in and seated in a double row on the opposite side of the court. The two accused were seated on the other side of the aisle at a table the same as ours, and were talking to their lawyer. We were all told to rise and the judge came in and took his seat.

My lawyer stood and stated the facts as they had happened and told the jury that he would prove that the defendants were guilty as charged. Their lawyer then stated the case for the defence. He told the jury that his clients were innocent of the charges and that they were there only on trumped-up charges and he would prove them to be innocent.

The first to give evidence was Allen, who said that we were going to the theatre and that I had left my bag containing the tickets in my car. As the car park was just round the corner I had gone to retrieve my bag and the tickets. After fifteen minutes they became worried and went looking for me. They found the car with the keys still in the door and my bag on the seat. He then contacted the police and waited for them to come to the car park. After the police had finished with the car they went looking round the streets for Miss North but found nothing. They had put Ben in a taxi because he was having difficulty breathing; the evening's experience had brought on an asthma attack, something to which he was very prone. Allen and Linda had then gone to Allen's flat and waited until they received a call to say that I had been found and was on the way to hospital. At the hospital they had found me in a distressed state and my face was badly bruised and my eye was already turning black.

The defence lawyer got up and started to cross-examine Allen. He asked, 'How long have you known Miss North, and how did you meet?'

'I have known her for just over a year, and the first time I saw her was when I successfully applied for a job in her company.'

'And what is your relationship now?'

'I have a good working relationship with her, and enjoy the job I am doing.'

'Are you trying to say that you never had a social relationship? After all, you say you were on the way to the theatre with Miss North.'

'Miss North invited us to the theatre to show her appreciation for the hard work we had put in with regard to a project we have been working on. It is not something that we have done before.'

'Have you ever been to Miss North's flat or she to yours?'

'Miss North has never been to my flat, there has never been the need for her to do so. And yes, I have been to her house just once, that was after the remembrance service for her mother and father, who were killed in a plane crash. Her solicitor and the vicar were present.'

After the defence lawyer had finished with Allen, a short recess was called. I said to my lawyer, 'They're implying that Allen was my lover; there's nothing further from the truth.'

He said, 'He is trying to discredit you, but Allen played his part well. He had nothing to hide, and the jury believed him.'

After the recess Linda was next on the stand, and her account of the evening mirrored Allen's. She told the court that her greatest regret was that she had not accompanied me back to the car, as if she had, this would never have happened.

The defence lawyer stood looking at the floor for some time before saying, 'You seem to have a high regard for Miss North.'

'She is a good employer who treats all her staff well, and I enjoy my job.'

'I believe that you and Miss North often stay in one another's houses. Is that correct?'

Linda looked across at our table and my lawyer was on his feet, objecting to the line of questioning. The judge asked them to approach the bench, but I could not hear what was being said. When my lawyer sat down again the other one went back to Linda and said, 'This is a simple question. Please answer yes or no. Have you or have you not spent time with Miss North alone in each other's houses?'

Linda was red with rage and said, 'I will not answer that question with a yes or no.'

'I demand an answer; it is a simple question and all it needs is a simple answer.'

Linda was now near to tears and said, 'Yes, she has stayed at my house and I have stayed at hers, but...'

The defence lawyer looked at the judge and said, 'No further questions,' and walked back to his seat.

My lawyer asked if he could re-question the witness. He walked to Linda and said to her, 'Now in your own words tell the court the circumstances why you stayed at Miss North's house, and why she stayed at yours.'

Linda was now back in control of herself and replied calmly with a clear voice. 'When Miss North lost both her mother and father in a plane crash she stayed with me until she felt able to return to work. This was because she felt unable to return to the house where she had lived all her life with them. When she did return I stayed for two nights so she could start to get used to them not being there. And again I stayed the night before the memorial service for her parents at the church in Wallingford. This was on the Saturday, and I returned home on the Monday.'

'Are these the only times you had stayed with her or she with you?'

Linda said 'Yes,' and was excused.

The next witness supposed to take the stand was Ben, but he had been struck down with a very bad attack of asthma. Paramedics had been called to his flat and he had been rushed into hospital. And although he was home his doctor had sent a letter stating that he was not to be taken away from the oxygen cylinder that had been installed in his flat. His statement was read out in court, and was the same as Linda and Allen's. The defence lawyer told the judge that it was unfortunate that he was not in court because he had some important questions he wanted to put to him.

I could guess what those questions were, and I was glad for Ben's sake that he was not there. The judge called the two lawyers to the bench, and it was some time before they resumed their places, with the defence lawyer looking very angry.

While the next witness was being called and sworn in I leaned over and asked my lawyer what the defence lawyer had said to the judge. He said, 'He was not happy that Ben was not there because there were some important questions he wished to ask him.'

I said, 'I knew what they are: the bastard has found out that Ben is gay, and he wants to get that over to the jury. He has tried to make us all look cheap, but he has lost out with Ben.' My lawyer just looked at me and shook his head.

The next witness was the policeman who had been called to the car park. He gave the time the police were called and the time that they arrived at the car park. He told the court that they had met Linda, Allen and Ben waiting by my car. The car was unlocked and the keys were still in the open door, my evening bag was on the seat and nothing seemed to be taken from the car. The next three spaces were unoccupied and there was no sign of a struggle.

My lawyer asked, 'What material was the car park made of?'

'Rolled asphalt.'

'Would you expect to find any signs of a struggle on that kind of surface?'

'No.'

The defence lawyer asked one or two questions about the position of the car, and had the officer noticed that there was a security camera in the car park. The officer answered the questions and told him that he knew the camera was there, it had helped in the past with car theft and vandalism.

'Did the film from this camera show either of my clients attacking Miss North?'

'The film showed Miss North at her car and then the van pulling up beside it. A few moments later the van left the car park and Miss North was gone and the door to her car was open.'

'So the film never showed my client talking to Miss North, or Miss North getting into the van?'

The officer said, 'No, because the camera was on the wrong side of the van and never showed the side door.' He was then told he could stand down. The court was then adjourned until two o'clock and we went out for coffee and something to eat.

When we returned to the court the video from the car park camera was shown to the jury, in which I could be seen in a three-quarter-length dress walking to the car and unlocking it. I was leaning over to reach my bag from the passenger seat when the white van pulled up beside me, blocking out the view of me and my car. A short time later the van pulled away and my car was still there with its door open, but I was gone. The defence lawyer told the jury that it proved nothing: Miss North getting into the van of her own free will could not be seen, and the accusation that she was kidnapped could not be proved. He could not see why the film had been brought in as evidence in the first place.

Mr Wise was next and he told how he and his wife were driving to their home in Didcot when he saw Miss North in the road in a very distressed state and stopped to see what was wrong. 'When I approached her I could see by the lights of the car that her dress had been torn from her and she was holding the remnants around her body. Her left eye was almost closed and it looked as though she had been beaten around the face. I took Miss North back to my car where she was comforted by my wife, and then I called the police at Miss North's request on my mobile phone. We then sat in the car until a police car arrived shortly afterwards. My wife went with Miss North and sat in the police car. Shortly after that another police car arrived, and we drove in convoy to where the track to the open barn met the road. Then the first police car to arrive, with Miss North and my wife still on board, drove to the hospital, and I followed, leaving the second police car at the entrance to the track. While at the hospital both my wife and I gave our statements to the police.'

The defence lawyer then asked Mr Wise, 'Did you see or hear the men who had been accused of abducting Miss North?'

'No.'

'Did you see the white van?'

'No.'

'Apart from what Miss North told you, you have no idea what happened up to the time you found her. You can neither confirm or deny that Miss North went of her own free will, can you?'

'No.'

'No further questions.'

Mrs Wise more or less repeated what her husband had told the court. The defence lawyer then put the same questions to her, and she could do nothing but answer 'No' to all of them.

When the doctor who had examined me at the hospital took the stand, he told them that I had been brought in by the police and that I had been beaten on the left side of my head. The blow had been sufficient to render me unconscious, and I had suffered mild concussion. He had examined the rest of my body and found bruises and bite marks on my breasts. There had been bruising around my thighs, and a thin red mark had been found around the back of my neck. After tests he had found that intercourse had taken place. Although no semen had been found, lubricant used on condoms was present, and he believed that police forensics could tell what make was used. The hospital had also given the police swabs taken from around the bite marks on my breast, along with what remained of my clothes.

The defence lawyer asked, 'Was the skin broken on the side of the face that had been bruised?'

The doctor answered, 'No.'

'Then could the injury have been self-inflicted by falling against a hard object?'

'In my opinion it was caused by a blow with a fist, but I cannot rule out a fall.' There were no other questions.

The first day in court was brought to an end and was to be resumed at ten next day. I went with the lawyer and barrister back to Mr Stroud's office, where we talked over what had happened during the day.

I said, 'It looks as though the defence lawyer is trying to make out that I had gone with those men of my own free will, and he is getting that over to the jury as often as possible. At some time tomorrow it will be me that he will be asking questions, and if he starts to make me look a liar I am going to give him a piece of my mind.'

The barrister said, 'If he gets too aggressive, look at us and I will object to the line of questioning. If he persists, we will ask to approach the bench and have a word with the judge. But you must keep as cool as possible and not try and discredit the defence counsel yourself, as that will give the wrong impression to the jury.'

After the meeting Mr Stroud drove me back to my apartment. That night I did not sleep well; the thought of that man asking me questions kept me awake most of the night.

While I was having breakfast the next morning the phone rang; it was Allen, wishing me luck in court. I thanked him for the way he had given his testimony the day before, and then asked how Ben was. He said that Ben had had a bad night, and it looked as though he would be taken back into hospital later that day. They had told him that there was a new treatment for his complaint and had offered him the chance to try it, but at the same time they could give no guarantees as to the outcome. He then told me that there were no problems at the office that I should concern myself about, and he had everything in hand.

I dressed in a grey two-piece trouser suit with low black shoes and white blouse, and wore a small pair of pearl earrings. Linda rang to wish me all the best for the day, and not to worry about the office because it was all under control. As I replaced the receiver the doorbell rang, and it was Mr Stroud to take me back to the courthouse.

On the short drive there he asked me, 'How do you feel about taking the stand today?'

'I've been thinking about it all night and will be glad when it is all over.'

'You must remember what you were told yesterday, because your lawyer will be there for you if you want him.'

Again there was a group of newspeople waiting outside the court with cameras and microphones. Mr Stroud and two court officials hurried me past them, and again I never said a word. When I took my place beside the lawyer and barrister I noticed that the court was packed, and said to the lawyer, 'There seem to be more people here today than yesterday.'

His reply was, 'They are here because you are to take

the stand today, but don't worry about them. Just remember all we talked about last night and you will do just fine.'

First to take the stand was a police officer, who told the court that the police had recognized the van on the tape from the car park. He had gone with another officer to the home of one of the defendants, where they discovered the white van. They had obtained a search warrant prior to going to the address, and this was shown to the defendant. They had then called Forensics to do an inspection of the van, but had not touched it themselves. The defendant refused to answer questions and was taken into custody and driven to the station after Forensics had arrived on the scene. At the station the defendant gave his name and said that he had driven his mate and a girl to a spot near Didcot. When they arrived he had gone for a walk, and when he returned half a hour later the girl was gone and his mate was in the driver's seat and had driven the van back to a pub in Oxford, where they had gone for a drink. When asked if the girl had gone with them of her own free will, he had said that he did not know. After some time he gave the police the name of his mate, and the next day the man was picked up and questioned. He did not co-operate during questioning and was held in custody awaiting further investigations.

The defence lawyer asked, 'Did my client make a statement about what had happened on the night in question?'

'The defendant did not say or do anything. He only confirmed his name.'

'Was he asked if he required a lawyer at that time?'

'He was, but he would not reply. It was the next day he asked for a lawyer and you yourself came to the station. It was then he made a statement saying that the girl had gone with him of her own free will.'

'Did the police believe this statement to be true?'

'It is not my job to believe or disbelieve a statement. I only collect evidence.'

'My client said in his statement that the girl had got into the van of her own free will. Did you believe him?'

'That is for the court to decide. I only collect evidence.'

'If I told you that my client was telling the truth, would your answer be the same?'

'It would.'

There were no other questions.

The man from Forensics was next. He told how they had inspected the van, and had found both of the defendants' fingerprints inside and outside the van. After minute inspection they had found no prints that matched Miss North's prints, which they found odd. There were bales of rags in the back of the van, and amongst these were found small remnants of Miss North's clothing. Several strands of Miss North's hair were also found on the rags. Between the bales they had found a valuable gold and diamond cross on a broken chain which was later found to belong to Miss North.

My lawyer asked him, 'If Miss North had fallen inside the van and opened the door and escaped, would you expect to find fingerprints belonging to her on the van door?'

'Yes, both on and around the door; but there were none.'

The defence lawyer asked, 'How many days elapsed from the night in question before you conducted the examination?'

'Two days.'

'This is a work vehicle, and the side door is opened and closed many times a day. My client's prints were bound to be on every part of the van; might they have covered Miss North's prints?'

'If Miss North's prints had been on the van, there is no doubt that we would have found them.'

104

'Did you find my client's prints on the gold cross found in the van?'

'No, the only prints found on the cross were those of Miss North.'

'So she could have broken the chain herself while she was having fun in the back of the van?'

'By the remnants of her clothing it did not look that way.'

'It appears that you do not know modern women. No further questions.'

Now it was my turn. I took my seat and my lawyer asked me to recount what had happened on the night in question. I retold all that had happened from the time I left the theatre to the time I left the hospital.

'Did you go with the men of your own free will, or were you abducted?'

'I was abducted and did not even see the man who had grabbed me. But I did see the back of the driver's head before I was blindfolded. I told the police that the driver had dark short curly hair, and seemed to be smaller than the man holding me. The man holding me was powerful, and I could do nothing to get away from him.'

My heart pounded as the defence lawyer came up to me and stood very close. He turned to the jury and asked me, 'When was the last time you had intimate relations with a man?'

I was lost for words and looked to my lawyer, who was already on his feet. He said he objected to this line of questioning and it was not relevant to the case.

The judge called them both and they talked for some time, then the defence lawyer came back and stood in front of me.

'Were you at the time in a permanent relationship with anyone?'

Again I looked at my lawyer, who was on his feet again, objecting to the question.

The judge said he did not see where this line of questioning was going but instructed me to answer.

I said, 'I was not in any kind of relationship then or now. My work takes up all of my time, and that suits me fine.'

'And how long ago did your last relationship finish?'

I told him that it was none of his business and to ask me questions about the night I was abducted. My lawyer was on his feet again, and they both went up to the judge and talked for a long time.

When the defence lawyer returned he said, 'My client maintains that you talked to him and got into the van at his request and were happy to go with him.'

'I was grabbed from behind and dragged into the van. I never saw his face.'

'And yet my client maintains that not only did you have sex but you fully participated in the act and helped tear the clothes from your body.'

'I did not participate in anything, for I was knocked unconscious and did not come round until they had driven away, leaving me naked on the grass.'

'Was it not the case that you hit your head whilst leaving the van, thus rendering you unconscious?'

'No, I was knocked unconscious when I tried to fight that man off me when I was still in the van.'

This line of questioning went on and on; all the time he was trying to make me look cheap. And he kept saying that I had agreed to go with them and that I was as much to blame for what happened as his clients. Time and time again my lawyer stood up and objected to his questions, and he would just rephrase them to ask the same thing in a different way. It was almost one o'clock before he said, 'No more questions,' and I was able to go and sit back with my lawyer at his table.

17

Court was adjourned until two and we left to find a quiet place to eat. The lawyer and barrister congratulated me on the way I had handled the cross-examination; they told me that our side had now finished and it was the defence lawyer's turn to produce his witnesses.

I said, 'I'll never forgive that man for what he put me through while I was on the stand. It feels like he has raped me in public, and by God, one day I will get my own back on the bastard.'

When the court resumed the driver of the van was sworn in, and he gave his version of what happened that night. It was a complete fabrication of what actually happened, and made it look like he was only a taxi driver and had no knowledge of what went on in the back of the van. On the drive back to Oxford his mate did not seem excited or worried, and they had gone for a drink and a game of pool. He said that he could not believe his mate had just raped a woman, because he had been so calm.

My barrister and lawyer had their heads together all the time he was giving his so-called evidence. And now my lawyer rose to question the driver.

'Could you tell the court the reason for your trip to the car park and why you parked next to Miss North's car? After all, there were many other parking places.'

'We had been driving round and I wanted a rest, and parked in the first spot I found.'

'When you go for a drive round, is it usual for your mate to ride in the back of the van?'

'He was in the back having a lie down on the bales of rags. He'd had a hard day.'

'Then when you parked next to Miss North's car he did not know that she was there; or did you inform him that she was there?'

'No, he opened the door to come and sit up front with me, that's when I heard them talking and later they both got into the back of the van.'

'Does it not seem strange to you that Miss North should leave her bag in the car and the door open?'

'I don't know; maybe it shows how eager she was to come with us.'

'What did she talk about on the drive to Didcot?'

'I don't know what was said. I couldn't hear them, they were in the back and I had the radio on.'

'You told the court that after driving to Didcot you went for a walk. Did it not seem odd to you that Miss North was no longer in the van when you returned, and you left without her, even though you were miles away from anywhere?'

'If she wanted to get out and walk, that was nothing to do with me. I didn't ask her to come in the first place.'

My lawyer walked up very close to the driver and said, 'You wouldn't know the truth if it jumped up and bit you. You are under oath and have told the biggest pack of lies a court has ever heard.'

The defence lawyer jumped up and objected to the last statement, and the judge called both lawyers to the bench. When they returned my lawyer said he was withdrawing his last comments and there were no other questions.

The man who had raped me was next to take the stand. His name was Hasset and he was from a well-known family who lived on the Oxfordshire/Berkshire border. He had been well-educated, but he and his family never had a good relationship. He had left home and been living rough in Oxford and told the court he was temporarily unemployed. His account of what happened was the same as the driver's; it was almost word for word.

He also told the court, 'She almost knocked me over in her hurry to get into the back of the van with me. She was willing right up to the time we had finished having sex, then she went wild and jumped out of the side door of the van. It was then that she slipped and hit her head. I could see that she was not badly hurt and decided to leave her there; it was plain to see that she did not want to be with us any more.' He had gone for a drink in Oxford and had not thought any more about the incident until the police came and took him to the station. And he could not believe that these charges had been brought against him.

My lawyer went across the court and stood between Hasset and the jury. He said, 'Do you expect the jury to believe that Miss North, who was taking her employees to the theatre for the evening and was dressed for the occasion, of her own free will jumped into the back of an old van filled with bales of rags with a man she did not know?'

'Whether they believe me or not, I can only tell you what happened and the way it happened. Some of these young women go looking for men like me; it gives them a thrill.'

'You say that she willingly consented to everything that happened inside the van, so could you tell the court how her clothes were torn to threads and her neck was injured where the chain of her gold cross was broken while it was still round her neck?'

'She just went wild for a time and she did most of that herself. She was OK until we had finished, then she just

109

wanted to get away. I had had my fun, so who was I to try and stop her going?'

'You are telling the court that Miss North got up and opened the side door of the van and fell while getting out?'

'Yes, I can only tell you what happened.'

'The inside and outside of that van have been examined, and yet no trace of Miss North's fingerprints have been found anywhere. Would you explain this to the jury?'

'I have no idea, perhaps they got wiped off or something.'

'Mr Hasset, you will have heard the doctor tell the court that Miss North's body had many bite marks and bruises, and you did not seem to have any marks on you at all. After the scene you describe this seems strange. Could you enlighten the court why this was?'

'No woman would ever mark me, and if they tried it would be the worse for them.'

'I suggest that is exactly what did happen. Miss North lashed out at you when you ripped her clothes from her, and you hit her so hard on the side of the head that she became unconscious. While she was in this state you raped her and then you threw her out of the van and her clothes on top of her. You then drove away, leaving her in the middle of nowhere. Is that not the case?'

The defence lawyer was up and complaining that my lawyer was badgering the defendant and making allegations he could not prove. He asked that the last outburst from my lawyer be stricken from the record.

The judge said he could see no reason for the objection and would let it stand; he would also like to hear the defendant's reply to the allegations.

My lawyer said, 'Well, we are all waiting to hear your reply, Mr Hasset.'

'It was not like that, it was how I have told you. I did not hit the woman and I did not throw her out of the van.'

My lawyer said, 'I am sure that the jury has heard your explanation and in their own good time will come to the correct decision as to where the truth lies.' He turned to the judge. 'No further questions.'

Court was again adjourned until the following day, and Mr Stroud drove me home. I asked him, 'How can a man tell so many lies? Do you think the judge and jury believed him?'

'Some men live by telling lies, and in the end they believe them themselves. They even tell lies when they know that the people who they are being told to know they are lies. It is as though they can't help themselves. And as for the judge and jury, I think they are intelligent enough to see through all the lies that they have been told today.'

My lawyer had told me that they had only two more witnesses to bring to the stand and a verdict should be pronounced by the afternoon.

I said, 'I can't see the jury acquitting either of them, so what sentence do he think they will get?'

Mr Stroud said, 'They will go to prison, but I couldn't guess for how long. But if they never get out, that will be too soon.' He said he would pick me up at the same time in the morning, and I went up to the apartment and ran a bath and soaked for over a hour.

Today I have sat here by the window, looking out at the world passing by, going over the past, and the things that have happened in my short life. My story is almost told, and soon you will be up to date with the events of the past.

On Monday I shall be back in the office again after all this time here on my own. The thought frightens me, but now I have a game plan and I know what it is I must do. Tomorrow evening Allen will call and we will go to the gym again, I shall do better this time, for I have been doing the exercises the instructor gave me. And already my body feels much more supple and I do not ache all over the next day. I am not sure that Allen will keep it up, but I intend to get myself fitter than I have ever been. But now I shall have a light evening meal, then a bath and an early night.

It has just gone seven and the morning is already light. I have completed my exercises and had a shower. I have hardly finished my breakfast when Allen rings. 'I'll pick you up for the late session at the gym, and perhaps we can get a takeaway on the way back – it'll be better to eat afterwards than before going.'

'That sounds a good idea. We should get a bottle of wine to finish off the evening.'

'Can I bring my file on the drug company project? I've got as far as I could get, and it might be a good idea to contact the men at the ministry and ask them for their opinion.'

'I'll read what you have and go over it all with you next week.'

The court was packed the next morning: they knew that this was going to be the last day of the trial, and they hoped that the jury would bring in the verdict today. This was only the third day, but it felt like a lifetime to me, and the sooner it was over the better I might feel.

The first witness of the day was a young man who had been in the pub when the two defendants had gone in late on the night in question. He told the court that when they came in they had acted the same as normal. Neither had seemed excited or in any way stressed; he had played pool with Mr Hasset and he had not mentioned anything about where they had been or what had happened. In fact both of the men had acted normally. My lawyer asked a few questions, but really there was not much he could ask and soon the man was asked to stand down.

The last witness had also been in the pub and told the same story, practically word for word, as the last man; in fact, it sounded as though he was reading a script. My lawyer asked him the same questions as the last witness and then said he had no more questions.

These two witnesses had not taken very much time, and only the summing up was left; although it was only eleven o'clock, a recess was called for one hour. My lawyer and the barrister went off for a conference, and Mr Stroud and I found ourselves a cup of coffee. I said, 'I hope it will all be finished today, and then perhaps the press will leave me alone.'

'It should reach a conclusion this afternoon, but the judge may not sentence them today. That may have to wait until tomorrow.'

When we returned to the court my lawyer was the first to speak to the jury. He more or less told them that the defendants had told the court a pack of lies. Nobody could believe that Miss North in any way encouraged them, and she would certainly never have got into the van of her own free will. In all his summing up lasted forty minutes, and left the jury in no doubt as to the way they should bring back a verdict of guilty for both of them.

The defence lawyer went over the same ground he had covered right through the trial, insisting that I had encouraged them and then cried rape. I should be taking an equal amount of blame for what had happened, and that his clients should never have been brought to court in the first place. Nothing had been proven against his clients, and they should be allowed to walk from this court as free men. We listened to thirty-five minutes of this, and by the time he had finished the jury looked fed up to the back teeth. The judge had a few words for them, and then they were led away to a room to consider their verdict.

After almost two hours the jury was led back in, and after they had taken their seats the judge asked the foreman of the jury whether they had reached a verdict.

'We have.'

The judge asked for the verdict of kidnapping against the defendant Hasset.

'Guilty.'

The jury found the driver guilty as well. The judge asked for the verdict as to the charge of actual bodily harm against Hasset.

'Guilty.'

But the driver was found not guilty. The judge then asked for the verdict on the rape charge against Hasset.

'Guilty.' They found the driver guilty by default.

The defence lawyer got to his feet and complained to the judge about the verdict, saying that the driver had not touched Miss North so he could not be guilty of rape, and there would be an appeal against this verdict. The judge said he would adjourn until tomorrow, and would then pass sentence on both of the defendants. The court was cleared and the defendants were taken back to the cells. We returned to Mr Stroud's office to talk over all that had happened, and then I was driven home.

At ten o'clock the next morning we were all back in court to hear the sentencing of both men. The driver was the first, and the judge told him that if it had not been for his involvement on that evening the crime might never had happened. He gave the driver five years imprisonment for the kidnapping and four years for the assistance in the rape of Miss North, the sentences to run concurrently.

114

He then turned to Hasset and told him that he was an evil man who gave no thought to others. He had committed these offences for his own pleasure and gratification, with no thought of the consequences. For the kidnapping charge he gave Hasset five years imprisonment, plus two years for the grievous bodily harm and seven years for the crime of rape. Again, these sentences were to run concurrently. The two defendants and their lawyer were grinning at each other and shaking hands.

There was uproar from the packed courtroom. People shouted that the sentences were a disgrace to the justice system. Others booed and shouted at the judge to think again.

I looked at my counsel and said, 'At least Hasset will be in jail for fourteen years, and the driver for nine years. So why is everyone shouting?'

My barrister then pointed out, 'The sentences are all to run concurrently. With remission the driver will be out on the street in just over two years and Hasset in just over three years. I will be appealing against the leniency of the sentences.'

I had been expecting the men to receive long sentences and had not evaluated the judge's last comments. I was appalled, and thought back to the letter that had been sent to me just after it had happened. The last part stood out like a neon sign. I knew just how she felt, and my heart went out to her.

The judge ordered the court to be cleared, and after a long time everyone was gone, leaving just us seated at our table. The barrister said there would be a crowd waiting outside the court, who would expect a statement from me as I left. He had been making notes all the time we had sat there, and in the end gave me a sheet of paper on which he had made a statement for the press.

He said he would read it out and send them a copy later that day. He advised me to stand by him and say nothing. I said that would suit me just fine.

As we walked out of the court I could not believe the number of people outside, newspapermen and radio reporters and even a TV crew, all pushing microphones at me and asking for my comments on the verdict. My barrister read out what he had prepared and told them that I had nothing to add at this time, but would give them a written statement later.

With the help of two police officers we made our way to Mr Stroud's car. I was glad to be inside away from the flashing cameras, the microphones and the shouted questions. As we drove away I noticed that a few of the more persistent of the reporters were following us in other cars. When we arrived at the office we went straight inside and locked the door. After sitting down the three men started going over what had happened in court. I sat in a dazed, confused state, not knowing what to say or do and taking no part in their deliberations. After an hour the reporters were still waiting at the front entrance. Mr Stroud called a taxi to come to the rear of the building to take me home. He told me to leave it all to them and he would call me tomorrow and tell me what had been decided.

After returning home I just sat and cried, unable to believe the day I had just lived through. Even though the two men were now in prison the feeling of fear would not go away. Linda and Allen called, and both asked if they should come round and sit with me for a while. I said it would be better if they stayed away and leave me to try and sort things out for myself.

17

Over the next weeks and months I became more withdrawn. Although Mr Stroud rang with reports on how things were proceeding, and Allen called at least twice a day, I could not bring myself to leave the apartment, and it has been like that for the last six months.

That was until this week, when at last I left the safety of the apartment to go to the gym with Allen. This brings us right up to date: in a little while we shall be going to the gym again, and on Monday morning I will be back behind my desk at the office.

I see Allen's car pull up outside, and this time I run down the stairs and get to the front entrance door just as he is about to ring the bell.

'You seem eager tonight. Let's go and see if this torture chamber that professes to be a gym can slow you down.'

Ted is pleased with the progress I have made, and increases my exercises for this session. Allen has obviously not exercised since he was here last, and is soon sweating profusely. He sits out the last quarter of an hour but grins at me while I am still running on the treadmill. After showering we drive back to my place and he comes in for coffee.

Allen says, 'Ben has had a bad day, and I'd like to get back before it gets too late. Would you like me to pick you up on Monday?'

'No, I will drive in myself; that's if the car starts. If it refuses to go, I shall go on the bus.'

We walk to the door, and he says, 'It's good to see you back in the real world again. You'll find that a few things have changed on Monday, but I'm sure you'll approve.'

Saturday and Sunday are spent getting the paperwork that has accumulated over the last six months in order and taken down to my car. To my surprise it starts straight away and I go for a drive down to look at the river.

On Monday I dress and sit for a while at the window, looking at the view that has been my world for the past six months. At seven-thirty I am in the car, heading for the office. Pulling into the car park and parking in my allotted space, it feels as if I have never been away. Not two minutes later Allen's car stops beside me, his grin lighting up the morning.

He comes round to my door just as I am getting an armful of folders to take up to the office. 'Leave all that where it is, we can get someone to come and retrieve it later. Come and have a look round before the others get in.'

In the six months I have been away we have taken over all the top floor of the office block. The main security doors have been moved, and so has the reception area. Now we have to go to the left and to the right, and every office on the floor is now in use. When we enter my office it is plain to see that it has been cleaned and polished, and flowers are on the window ledge.

'Thanks, Allen. I can see that you and the team have worked hard, and now it's time for me to start pulling my weight.'

Walking to the safe by the side of my desk, he takes out some folders and places them on the desk. 'This is the little project I have been working on, and I'd like you to look it over and give me your comments. I'll call back later and introduce you to the new staff you now have to pay.' With that he is gone.

Before I can open any of the folders there is a knock and Linda's head appears around the door. She comes in and gives me a hug and tells me how nice it is to have me back with them. She looks at the folders on my desk and says, 'That looks like a busy start to your return.'

'It's something Allen has asked me to look over, and I suppose I had better start earning my bread if I'm going to be allowed to stay.' Linda laughs and leaves me to it.

Using the code that is in the folder I bring up the program on the computer. It is not long before I can see that Allen is targeting only projects that have been worked on by the pharmaceutical industry for many years – areas where millions of pounds have been wasted by many companies doing the same research yet still achieving few or no results. He concludes that the financial side of finding and supplying expertise in each individual field and the time to get each company to work for a shared reward would not pay us for the cost of setting it up and the running of it, but if we could negotiate a percentage of the profits gained from new drugs found through the enterprise, the profits will by far outweigh our costs.

At midday Allen comes in to see me and says it is about time for me to meet all the new staff. The numbers have now increased to twenty-four, and although I know their names from the pay records, many of them have never seen me, or I them. It is strange to put faces to the names of people I have been paying for many months. Every department we go into seems to be busy, and our little tour takes most of the afternoon. By the end I have spoken to everyone and know what part they play in our organization. I tell them all that they will soon get used to me, as they will now see me every day. And my office door is always open if anyone needs to talk. This includes things outside of office matters.

Back in my office I tell Allen to sit down. 'I am amazed

by the way we have grown while I have been sitting at home, Allen. By all that I have seen today it seems impossible that you have found time to organize the workload and the layout of the extended office. You must have burned a lot of midnight oil to prepare this new project, which has taken me all morning to read through.'

Allen gives his little grin and says, 'You've only met the daytime staff.'

This seems strange because I have just met everyone on our payroll. 'Who is the phantom member of staff, and where do his wages come from? We don't deal in cash, so they cannot be paid on the side. And you know that I wouldn't allow it anyway.'

'Look,' says Allen, 'you know Ben and his long-standing problem with asthma, and how he has been out of work for a very long time. He is now undergoing a new course of treatment, and he seems to be much better. He gets very bored just sitting at home all the time, so he has been coming back to the office with me in the evenings. And it is with his help that so much has been achieved. I can assure you that the agency files have not been accessed once in all the time he has been here, so there is no chance of a security risk in any way. I admit to you that I did use the agency database to find the best specialist in the country, and used your name to get him to treat him – and he is now doing so at very special rates. I hope you will forgive me.'

'Look, Allen, this just will not do! How could you let Ben come here night after night for no reward? How many hours a week does he work, it has to be at least twelve or maybe fifteen a week? You will put him on the payroll as part-time staff, and he will be paid half of our usual salary, with all the benefits. I presume that you are paying the cost of this treatment he is getting; that will stop as from now because, as from this moment, the firm will cover all the costs. Do I make myself clear?

'While we are on the subject of work, in my eyes you have been the manager around here for some time, and that has to change too. As from the beginning of the month you will be a partner, not an employee. I will see my solicitor tomorrow and transfer five per cent of the company into your name. You will not only receive your salary, but will also receive five per cent of the profits at the end of each year. I cannot say what the figures will be until I have spoken to the accountants. Now what have you got to say?'

Allen just sits and said nothing for some time, so I wait for him to reply.

'It's impossible for me to comment on what you have offered me. Maybe tomorrow it will have sunk through my thick skull, and then perhaps we can talk again.'

When Allen leaves the office I close down the computer and lock all the papers in the safe. It is getting late, and it has been a long day for me. As I leave I can hear Allen talking to Ben on the phone as I pass his office door, and hope that I have done the right thing.

On the way home I stop at the supermarket, and for the first time in six months do my own weekly shopping. Walking around the store I find many things that had been forgotten for a long time, and by the end the trolley is full to the top. After driving home and putting all the shopping away, I realize that if this is going to be consumed in a week, I shall have to visit the gym more often.

The rest of the week passes quickly and I am soon back in the swing of things. By Friday I have got to know the new staff and they have had time to get to know me. Although my time is fully taken up, I still find time to ring Mr Stroud at his office and explain the arrangement I want drawn up to give Allen a share in the business. I also call the accountant so I can let Allen know the value of his shares and what he can expect at the end of the financial year as his share of the profits. Both are surprised by my decision, but when I explain they understand my reasons. I tell Allen it will be the end of the month before the paperwork will be ready.

The next Wednesday Allen takes me to the gym again. I have a good workout and asked if I can come again on Friday. Allen looks at me aghast, so I tell him that I will be coming on my own unless he cannot keep away.

'If you are now happy to come on your own, that's fine by me, but I may still come on Wednesdays if that's OK with you. The exercise seems to do me good, and now I've started it would be a shame to give up.'

After coffee at my apartment he thanks me again for the offer. 'I haven't been expecting anything, and this is unbelievable.'

I ask how Ben is. 'Is he still only coming to the office in the evenings?'

'He's fine, but he hasn't been to the office this week; he's been working on the folders at home.'

'There's nothing to stop him coming during the day; your office can stand another desk, and it will be better to have everything at hand.'

He thanks me again and is gone.

At the end of the month I have settled back into office routine and am pulling my weight in the day-to-day running of things. Mr Stroud has drawn up the partnership agreement between Allen and me, and my accountants now have all the figures worked out for me. It comes as a shock to me when I see the valuation placed on the company, which is a seven-figure amount. They tell me this is a conservative amount and if I wish to put the company on the market, I can expect much more.

On the first of the next month I drive Allen to Mr

Stroud's office to sign the papers. Mr Stroud reads them through to us and passes them over to us to sign. It is the first time Allen realizes just how much his share amounts to, and he sits there with his mouth open and does not say anything.

'Come on, Allen,' I say, 'put your mark there and let's get back to work.'

He signs his name and we leave the office and walk back to my car. We are almost back to our office before he says anything.

'You must think me very rude, but it never crossed my mind that it would be such a large amount.'

'Look, Allen, you have earned every penny, but if you want to sell out you have to remember you must give me the first offer to buy your share back; or to sell only to someone I approve of.'

'I can never see the time when that will happen, Jack. I must be the luckiest man alive.'

Now you know how I came to be here, and I can tell my story as it happened from this point.

18

I waited until the New Year before starting to prepare
for what I had in mind for Mr Madden, who handled the
defence of the two men at the trial. It had taken that
long to find the right private investigator to carry out
the task that I was about to embark upon. His name was
Kirk Weston and he was an ex-policeman. He charged by
the day and never gave guarantees, but he was the best,
and his reports were in my letter box every Friday without
fail.

The information required was a list of all the cases and
clients that Madden had taken on, especially those that
involved rape or indecent assault on women. I also wanted
as many past court transcripts he had handled involving
rape or indecent assault. When I asked if Kirk thought
we could get someone into his office as a secretary so
we had someone on the inside, he said that might be
impossible and probably illegal as well, but we could
always look at other options later. He was being paid
from my private account, and he was only to contact me
at home, never at work.

Now I am attending the gym twice a week, and it feels
good to be back in shape again. Ted has also enrolled
me in a martial art and self-defence course that is run
by his brother Ken in the same building. Ken is a little
older than Ted, but they look like twins with their bald

124

heads and very muscular bodies. I have been attending his classes for some time and seem to be progressing well; Ken has asked me if I would like to enter a few competitions, but I have told him that I am not interested. 'What I am doing here is for my own piece of mind.' He smiles one of his rare smiles but keeps me working hard, and still shouts when I get things wrong. I love them both dearly, but would never tell them so.

Each day at work brings new problems to solve and new sections of the healthcare system to investigate. The team we have are now finely tuned and deal easily with things we used to struggle with. Allen is a rock, and although he is still working on his own project with Ben's assistance, he is always there to give his advice and time when needed. I cannot think what I should do without him.

Many hospitals and even private clinics now use our database on a day-to-day basis. They have found that the fees they pay to us outweigh the cost of their own administration, and it is much quicker. If they are looking for specialists or ambulance drivers, these can all be found within our record system. The company is well established now, but there are still things to do to make it run more smoothly. But then again, there always will be.

Kirk Weston's reports were arriving at my apartment each Friday, sometimes on Wednesdays as well. The amount of information he was passing on to me was staggering. He had also managed to get a cleaner installed at Madden's office; he did not think that it would bring much information, but the chances were there.

He had managed to get eleven transcripts of past cases involving rape or indecent assault; these proved very interesting, and I spent many hours studying them. In the end I had a pile of folders all in order and highlighted with marker pens at the relevant passages. For I found that he used the same questions in nearly all the cases: these were only to make the witness look bad in the eyes of the jury, even though they had no direct bearing upon the case.

The list of cases in which Madden was representing rape or indecent assault clients seemed to grow by the week. These I listed in order of seriousness, and the names of the victims' solicitors handling the prosecutions printed on each folder. To these I sent copies of the highlighted transcripts, and a covering letter giving the reasons for doing so, pointing out that it would improve the chances of a good result if they knew in detail what to expect from the defence beforehand.

Some wrote to thank me before trials started, but nearly all wrote after the trials to say how much help the information had been. Over the next two months Madden lost every case he was involved with, some of them badly. Kirk Weston said that if things went on like this, Madden would be out of business. I told him that I wanted him in jail, and that I was sure that the way he operated was in the most part illegal.

Then Kirk Weston had a real bit of good fortune. It appeared that Madden was having a clear-out at his offices. The cleaner we had working there was told to remove some plastic bags of rubbish, which were duly delivered to Kirk and then to me. They consisted of not only papers, but notebooks and, most importantly, tape recordings. The sorting of this was a never-ending task, and it was not long before my home resembled a rubbish tip. Much of it did not mean a thing to me, but these items were put back in plastic bags, as they might come in useful later on.

Then came the break I was looking for: the rough notes

that had been taken when he was interviewing the two men who had kidnapped and raped me, and a tape recording he had made of that interview. As soon as I realized what I had found it was important not to handle any item that might show fingerprints, such as notebooks with smooth covers and tape cassettes. Both the notes and tape showed that the men had admitted to Madden that they were guilty of all the charges. Madden had then told them the exact statement to make, and indicated that if his instructions were followed to the letter the sentences would be light. It was Madden who orchestrated the lies that were eventually heard by the jury.

All of this I gave back to Kirk Weston and asked if he could get the handwriting verified as Madden's, and to have the voice checked so we could prove that it was his. He told me that if I was going to take this to the police, it should be they who do the fingerprinting. As he pointed out, we must leave them something to do.

Kirk must have had some good contacts, because he was back in less than a week. In both cases the match was certain.

Kirk said, 'The man must be completely mad to have kept all this in his office. Had he wanted to dispose of it he should have burnt it all, and he should have done it himself. You wanted him struck off and put away; well now you have all the evidence to do just that. But remember that someone sent these records to your apartment. Whatever you do, don't tell them that you employed me to get them for you. What we have done is not quite legal, but if they don't know who sent them they can't complain.'

After putting all of the items in order and rereading everything, I made an appointment to see Mr Stroud at his office. He was pleased to see me and asked what my problems were. I told him that a package had been delivered to home with no covering letter. After explaining the contents of the package, I told him how careful I had been not to remove any fingerprints from anything. If this was sent to our barrister, it might help to alter the sentences of the two men who were now in jail.

He read through the papers and we listened to the tape. He looked at me and said he did not know about the two men in jail, but he thought that Madden could well be joining them. He rang the barrister and had a long conversation with him. He then played the tape to him over the phone, and it was a long time before the barrister spoke again. At last he said he would see to it right away and rang off.

Mr Stroud asked a lot of questions, to which I managed to keep my answers guarded but very near to the truth. When we had finished I returned home.

The next five weeks were very busy at the office, and I had little time to think about anything else. Allen still joined me at the gym for one session a week. And I still attended the martial art classes. By now all the exercise was showing in how I felt and the way I looked, I was fitter now than I had ever been. And I intended to keep it that way. Then one Friday evening there was a phone call from Mr Stroud. He wanted me to meet him in his office on the following Tuesday morning. The barrister would be there plus one other, but he would rather not talk about it over the phone. When the call was finished I sat and wondered what the next move would be.

Sunday morning found me walking along the side of the Thames with Kirk Weston. We went over all that I had told Mr Stroud and the information he had relayed to the barrister while I was in his office. I explained that nothing had been said about the voice recognition or that we had checked on the handwriting, but I had been careful not to remove any fingerprints that might be on any of the items. Kirk said, 'It looks as though your barrister intends to take Madden to the cleaners. You'll be back in court to see him get his comeuppance.'

When I arrived Mr Stroud's office was full of people: Mr Stroud and his secretary, the barrister and his secretary, and a man I had not met before, who turned out to be from the Crown Prosecution Service. It was plain to see that I had stirred up a hornet's nest.

The meeting went on for over two hours, and the barrister asked me many questions about the items I had delivered to them. I gave the same answers I had given to Mr Stroud, and in the end asked if they thought the two men who kidnapped me would have their sentences altered. Now that the court could see that their defence was based on a pack of lies, it must make a difference.

To this I was told that this might well be the case. But the Crown Prosecution officer was more interested in the part that Madden had played in orchestrating those lies. The notebooks and tapes had been analysed, and there was no doubt that the writing and voice on the tapes were those of Madden. His fingerprints were found on all of the items, and when he was questioned he could not deny it. The Crown Prosecution Service was preparing a case against him for knowingly perverting the course of justice, and encouraging others to do the same. If successful it would mean a long term in jail. The case was also being sent to the Bar Council, and if they ruled against him he would be disbarred and would never be able to get back into his profession. They thanked me for coming and said that if and when it got to court they could see no reason for me to be called.

Before I left I took another tape from my bag and gave it to the barrister, saying, 'This came with the other papers and did not appear to have anything to do with my case, but it seemed to be the same voice, I should have brought

129

it with the rest but I forgot.' It was difficult to keep the smile from my face as I left to go back to work.

That evening I rang Kirk Weston and asked him to call at my apartment as soon as he found time to do so.

'What have you in mind now?'

'I want you to collect the bags of papers and tapes that are still here. I am sure that you will know what to do with them, and I will see that you do not lose out for all your assistance.'

I heard him laugh, and the next evening he duly collected them.

Over the next two months our workload increased, and after talking it over with Allen we decided to take on two more staff. We no longer advertised for staff, but used our own records to find the people with the skills that we required. After contacting a few people, we would select those who fitted our requirement best from those who were willing to come to us. We now occupied the entire top floor of the building, and with the extra personnel it was clear that more space would soon be necessary. Allen and Ben's project had ground to a halt, and although we kept the files open, progress was very slow. Ben was now working more on our side than on the other project, but he again fitted in well with the others.

Our office was now open on Saturdays with a reduced staff, and also Sundays with a skeleton staff. Linda had now been promoted to senior supervisor, and she, Allen and myself took it in turns to be there. This particular Saturday it was my day off, and after a leisurely breakfast I was opening the mail. There was a letter from Mr Stroud informing me that Madden had been suspended from practising law pending the trial, which would start next week. The irony was that the case would be held in the same court that I had attended, and although I was not to be called as a witness, he thought I might wish to attend.

On Monday I told Allen and Linda that I would like the rest of the week off. After I explained the reason, they both smiled and wished me luck. Tuesday found me in the court early; it surprised me to see so many women in the court, but I found a good seat. The charge against Madden was that of knowingly perverting the course of justice, and advising and assisting others to do the same; to the charges he entered a plea of not guilty. The addresses to the jury took up almost the whole of the morning, and when they were finished the court was adjourned until after lunch.

In the afternoon the first witness was a fingerprint expert who stated that the prints on the covers of the notebooks and the cassettes were those of Mr Madden. The defence lawyer asked a few inconsequential questions but never made any real headway. The next up was a young woman who was a handwriting expert, who stated that the writing in the notebooks and other papers was definitely that of Mr Madden. She had two boards set up in the court with enlarged copies of writing taken from the evidence and that obtained from Madden. She pointed out the similarities in a dozen different places and said that this could not be coincidence; in her opinion, there was no doubt that Madden had written them all. Again the defence had very little to say. In fact, there was nothing he could say. At this point the court was adjourned until Wednesday.

Next day in court I recognized many of the women who had been there the previous day; and by the time that court proceedings started, most of the seats were taken. Next to take the stand was a voice recognition

131

expert, who stated that he had analysed the tapes and compared his findings with a taped interview he had taken from Madden. In his opinion there could be no doubt that the findings pointed to the fact that the voices were the same. He also had a graph showing how he had come to his conclusions. This time the defence lawyer took his time over the cross-examination., asking many questions that to me never made sense. It looked to me that he was just trying to justify his expenses. Madden just sat there watching, and never communicated with his defence counsel at all. When this witness stood down, that was the end of the prosecution's case.

Two witnesses for the defence were a handwriting specialist who in the end had to admit that the chances of Madden writing the papers were eighty per cent positive. Next came a voice expert, who said that although there were many similarities in the tapes, he was not one hundred per cent certain it was Madden's voice. He was then asked how he thought Madden's fingerprints came to be on the tapes. The defence lawyer objected to the question, and the prosecution just said no more questions and sat down.

The final two witnesses were Hasset and the van driver, who had been brought from prison. It was a shock to see them again. Both insisted that their interview with Madden had not been taped, so the tapes had to be fake. When asked about the notes taken at the interview, both insisted that they could not recall what had been said at that time.

Madden himself had elected not to take the stand, which surprised me. After the summing up the case was given to the jury, who retired. There was not long to wait, and two hours later they filed back into court. When the verdict of 'Guilty' was read out, a cheer rang round the court and the judge had difficulty in restoring order. He then said that Madden would be brought back to court for sentencing on Monday morning.

As I left the court a small crowd of women were shaking hands, all seeming to be talking at once. After listening to them for a while it dawned on me that they had all suffered at Madden's hands, and that notes and tapes had been mailed to them from some unknown source, with instructions to send them on to the public prosecutor. Kirk Weston had certainly earned his fee.

The following Monday I was in the front row in court to hear Madden sentenced to six years in prison. No doubt he would be out in three, but he will never practise law again.

A few weeks later I had a call from Mr Stroud to tell me that after the appeal the light sentences handed out to Hasset and the van driver had been increased. The fact that they had supported Madden had not helped their cause, and now it looked as though Hasset would not be back on the streets for at least five years. I hoped that this would bring an end to the nightmare I had lived for all this time.

This all happened three years ago, and now I am the self-confident person of old, knowing that I had the ability to defend myself against anyone who thought I was a pushover. It was good to socialize again and go to concerts and shows. I gained a few male followers whose company I enjoyed, but still slept alone in my own bed every night – and I liked it that way.

18

Over this period we had not expanded the business interest, but had fine-tuned every aspect of what we were doing. Most of the communications in and out of the office were electronic, but the daily postbag was still heavy. Ann, our receptionist, sorted the mail and had it delivered to the relevant departments; very little of it ever landed on my desk, therefore it surprised me to find a large envelope on my desk marked 'For Miss J. North's eyes only', and carrying a Swiss postage stamp.

It was from a company that specialized in obtaining control of firms by negotiating for interested clients. From reading through all the papers it became apparent that they had gone to a lot of trouble in collecting their information. But it was also plain to see that they had not breached our security, and this gave me a lot of pleasure. It was over two hours before I called Allen into the office, and gave him the letter to read through.

When he had finished reading I asked him for his thoughts.

'Well, it looks like they have gathered a lot of information about us, but have not managed to get through our security. None of what they say has come from our secure files. There is no indication as to who they are working for, or from which country they might come. And no mention of the figure to indicate the value they put on the company, but I suppose this is only the first contact with us on the matter.'

'Do we answer the enquiry or sit back and wait? I have never dealt with anything like this, and to be honest, I have never even thought about it. But it does look like a genuine enquiry. Even though I am not sure that I would want it to go to anyone else, I suppose we should make some reply while giving them no indication as to the way we are thinking.' With that I suggested we went out to lunch and composed a reply when we got back.

On our return we drafted out a reply and then went over it together. It was more difficult than we first thought. It had to be the right mix, neither wanting to reject them out of hand but also not appearing to be eager to take the offer further. What we wanted was more information on who the people involved were, and why the offer was being made. It was after five o'clock before we had something that we both thought was right, and I locked it all in the safe and prepared to leave for home. Walking to our cars, Allen said, 'I think we should keep this to ourselves for the time being, don't you?'

'Yes, the fewer who know about it the better. But we will go over it all again tomorrow before we send the reply.'

The next morning I was in early and was not surprised to find Allen there as well. He said, 'I've been turning it over most of the night, and have come to the conclusion that maybe we should take some professional advice before doing anything.'

'That makes sense, but I have no idea who to ask. Perhaps if we had a word with Mr Stroud; at least he is a man we can trust.' Allen agreed.

I called Mr Stroud and made a appointment for two o'clock, and I told him that Allen would be with me. The rest of the morning was hectic, and there was no time to talk to Allen until it was time to go.

After being shown into the office and taking a seat,

Mr Stroud asked if we wanted his secretary to take notes. Looking at Allen I shook my head, and he said, 'Maybe later, but not right now.'

She left the room and Mr Stroud sat with his hands on his desk and said, 'Now then, tell me what is worrying you two?'

I said, 'Allen and I have received a letter, and before we make a reply we both thought it wise to come and see you. I think you should read it first and then we can talk it through afterwards.'

Allen pushed the envelope across the desk towards him, and said, 'There are very few people we thought it wise to trust. This is why we have come to you.'

After reading it through, Mr Stroud looked up and said, 'I see your point. Has this enquiry come out of the blue, or have you been putting out feelers?'

Allen said, 'This is out of the blue, and although they appear to know a lot about us, we are positive that our security had not been breached.'

I added, 'We feel that a reply should be made, but giving no commitments either way. This is because we don't know quite how we feel about the idea of selling to another party. We would like to talk to someone who could deal with the situation, as whatever we do must be done right.'

Allen said, 'We were hoping that maybe you know someone to advise us. It's not the thing we want bandied about, as that may affect the confidence our clients have in us.'

'When your father sold his company,' said Mr Stroud, 'he had a firm of negotiators handle the sale, and I got to know the man who handled it quite well. I have his name on file, and if you want me to contact him just say the word and we can ring him now.'

Allen looked at me and then asked if we could have a

136

few minutes alone to talk it over. Mr Stroud said he would go and see about getting a coffee for us, and left the room.

'What do you think, Jack?' said Allen. 'It all seems to be going so fast, and I don't know about you, but I'm having difficulty keeping up.'

'Look, Allen, we didn't ask for this and we don't know where it will lead. We mustn't look as though we are or are not interested in the proposal. It won't hurt to talk to this man who handled Daddy's sale, and he might give us some good advice.' I could see that Allen was out of his depth, and I don't mind admitting that I was too. 'But we should ask Mr Stroud to come back in and phone his contact and ask when he can meet us; it can do no harm to talk.'

When Mr Stroud got through he said, 'Hello, Donald, this is Stroud; remember, you handled a sale for Mr North a few years back. Well, now his daughter would like some advice and I recommended she come to you.' They chatted for some time and Mr Stroud outlined the type of company that we ran and the fact that a Swiss firm had made overtures to us and seemed to be looking to acquire the company for a third person. He then switched the phone on to the speaker so that Allen and I could hear the conversation.

The man introduced himself as Donald McNee, and after talking for some time he recommended that we make a reply acknowledging receipt of their letter and saying that they would be contacted again in a few days. 'In the meantime we should meet, perhaps at your office, or perhaps we could all intrude on Mr Stroud.' Allen and I thought our office would be best because all the records were kept there, and it might be handy if they were needed. McNee said he would check on a few things on Tuesday and meet us on Wednesday morning.

137

Back at the office, the first thing we did was to send off our reply acknowledging receipt of their letter. Before leaving, Allen and I decided to come in early on Tuesday and sort out the paperwork that Mr McNee might need to see on Wednesday. It should not take long, but it would be better if we did it before the rest of the staff got in.

By the time the staff arrived next day we had sorted out what we thought might be needed and Allen was back at his desk. Mr McNee was not expected until ten, so I tried to do some routine tasks until he arrived. He was in fact a little early and Allen escorted him into my office. We had laid out the papers that he might need on the spare desk, so I sat him down and ordered coffee for three to be brought in. Before the coffee arrived Linda stuck her head round the door and said to us that we had better come quickly.

19

We could all hear telephones ringing in the outer offices, and before I reached the door the one on my desk was ringing too. Allen went out into the other offices and I snatched up the receiver from my desk phone. I listened with horror at what I was being told, and in the end I said that we were dropping everything and would deal only with this until I heard from him again.

Remembering Mr McNee, I turned to him and said, 'I'm sorry but our talk must be cancelled. There's been a disaster and we will be flat out for the foreseeable future. You can look through the things on the desk at your leisure, but now I must join the others and get things moving.'

'Can I ask what has happened and if I can help?' he said.

'There's been a rail accident involving a passenger train and a tanker lorry transporting liquid gas. The tanker exploded on impact and there are as many as three hundred casualties. Nine hospitals have been alerted, and this will mean that for some time we are going to be very busy indeed. I have promised the man from the Ministry that we will give it our full attention.'

In the outer offices everyone was either on the phone, taking faxes or bringing up information on computer screens. All the personnel were working flat out but it gave me pleasure it see that there was no panic; they were doing the job that they had been trained to do. For two hours there was little time to think of anything else. But after that things began to cool down a little, and I returned to my office to find Mr McNee still there.

While I sat at my desk and wrote out an initial report on the ongoing operation he sat there in silence. When I had finished he handed me a cup of coffee he had managed to get from somewhere. I really looked at him for the first time. He was about my age but looked several years older, good-looking in an odd sort of way, with wavy hair that refused to stay in place – the type of man that you would expect to find walking the moor or birdwatching or messing about in the garden, not the office type at all. When he spoke his voice was soft with a Scottish lilt, which was pleasant to listen to.

'Sorry you have had a wasted day, Mr McNee, but this is why we are here: when the call comes through, we have to act. In the last two hours we have mobilized nine ambulances and twenty-three paramedics, eleven burns specialists and extra nurses with burns expertise, not to mention extra medical staff and trauma specialists, as well as counsellors. That's a hundred and sixteen in all, but three will not be at the hospitals for another hour because two are coming from France and one from Germany.

'Now that the initial rush has been seen to, Allen and six of the staff will be going home to sleep. The rest of us will be here until midnight, and then Allen and the others will be back in to relieve us and be on call through the night. In the meantime we must catch up with the routine work of the day.'

'This was not a good time to come, but I'm glad I did. I will not take up any more of your time, but I would like you to listen to me for a moment. I did some research yesterday into the proposal you received, and have read through the papers you have supplied me with. I will tell you now that there are two more very large players looking

140

at your enterprise. It will not surprise me if there is interest shown from them in the next week or two. If you would let me know the way you intend to proceed, I would be willing to handle it for you.'

I thanked him for coming and told him we would make another appointment in a day or two; in the meantime we would keep him fully informed of any new developments.

A week later we were still getting requests connected with the rail crash, but now they were being dealt with in the normal way. In total we had dealt with almost three hundred requests that were directly linked to the crash. It gave me great pleasure when we received a letter from the Minister of Health, thanking all the staff for the part we had played in the aftermath of the disaster. This I had copied and personally delivered to all our employees.

Allen and I sent a letter to Mr McNee telling him to act for us in regard to the Swiss inquiry, asking him to establish what it all entailed and what value they placed on our company, but to give no commitment on our part.

About a year previously we had asked the Ministry of Defence if they would consider entering their medical personnel onto our register. At the time they declined on the grounds of national security. After the rail crash I was taken aback to receive a request asking if they could now be included in our register, but asking if it was possible to keep all the information separate from the civil register. Allen pointed out that it would be expensive to set up, and only a limited number of staff would be able to have access to the information. I could see his point and we decided to have formal talks with the Ministry before taking it any further.

Two weeks after the day of the train crash two letters arrived on my desk, one from the Swiss people asking for a meeting to discuss their proposals, and the other from a German firm stating they had clients interested in acquiring our company. It would appear that Mr McNee had been right in his speculations. After talking it over with Allen, I rang McNee to tell him what was happening. He said it was not unexpected, and we arranged to meet the next day.

Mr McNee was early again and we all shut ourselves in my office. The first thing he said was that his name was Donald and he would be pleased if we used it. I told him my name was Jackie, and he already knew Allen.

Donald said, 'The first thing I need to know is have you decided what you want to do?'

Allen looked at me and said, 'Before anything can happen, we need to know exactly what it is they are offering us. It is obvious that we have something they want, but could this not be a trick to get into our files and steal the records that we have accumulated? We pride ourselves that the security in this office is the best in the country, and we sure as hell are not going to give that all away.'

Donald removed from his briefcase two folders and gave us one each. 'Now we will go through these page by page,' he said, 'and discuss each part on its merits after you have read what they contain.'

The first page gave us the identity of the company represented by the Swiss firm. It was a German concern based in Mannheim who dealt in Public Relations, and had interests worldwide. In the past three years they had diversified and now had dealings in manufacturing and distribution.

The second was another German company, this time based in Antwerp, Belgium. This one seemed to be into everything: shipping looked to rank high along with air travel and air freight, but this company was into many other enterprises as well.

Allen was the first to speak, and he voiced my thoughts as well. 'They both look solid and well-established concerns, but I still can't see why they would be looking at us.'

'You are the only player in this field in the UK; there is nothing to come remotely close to what you have achieved. Just imagine if what you have was expanded to cover all of Europe. Your recipe for success has been proven, and the information you hold is secure and can be quickly recovered. This is what makes your company a prime target. Now read the next page; it may come as a shock to you both.'

This was more information on the company in Mannheim, including the expected enlargement of our operation and the number of personnel needed to run it. It was the figure they had budgeted for the acquisition of our company that made my and Allen's mouths drop open. It was twenty million pounds sterling, a truly staggering amount. We sat there and could think of nothing to say.

Donald broke the silence and told us that in his opinion this was a conservative figure, which did not help. He had not managed to get the figures from the Antwerp Company, but thought they would be about the same. 'I must also point out to you that if you decide to carry on as you are, you must break out and get onto the Continent as soon as possible. If you don't, then you will be always looking over your shoulder in the future. Now they have you in their sights, they will not let go.'

It was getting near midday so I asked Donald if he would mind if we went to lunch. 'I think it best if Allen and I eat by ourselves – we need to talk this over, and we will meet back here at two o'clock.'

Allen and I went to a pub near the office and found a table in a quiet corner where we could talk. When the food came, both of us pushed it around the plates and ate very little. I sipped a glass of white wine and Allen had a small beer.

'I never thought it would come to this,' he said at last. 'I was happy with the way things were going; now I don't know what to think.'

'Allen, you know as well as me that I do not need the money, but do you want to see someone break into our database and steal everything that we have worked for? From the way Donald was talking they will get in sooner or later, and then it will all have been for nothing. Plus the fact that your share of what is on offer will amount to a million pounds – you wouldn't want to lose that.'

'It's not the money, it is the fact that I have never been happier in my life. And if we sell, what do I do for the rest of my life?'

'You could always resurrect your own file. That's not part of the company as far as I am concerned; it belongs to you and Ben. And with the money you are going to get properly invested, you will have a good standard of living without working.'

'You're probably right. Let's get back to the office and see what assurances he can give us as regards to the employees before we get this underway.'

Getting back to the building we found Donald sitting in his car waiting for us, so we all went up to my office together. When we were all seated I told Donald that we had decided that although it looked better for us to let someone else take over our enterprise, there would be commitments that would have to be guaranteed, mostly to do with our staff, such as wages, pensions, holidays and working conditions.

Allen then pointed out that there might be difficulty with some government departments. 'The two that spring to mind are the department that deals with Data Protection and the Ministry of Health, but there may well be others.

If these other companies were based in this country, I feel that it would be much easier for all concerned. You should know that the Ministry of Defence had made application to be entered on our register, but we haven't taken the matter any further.'

Donald then told us that he had only told us of the two where he had proof of their interests. 'There are more, but I could not commit myself at this moment. Where the Ministry of Defence is concerned, I think that you should hold off for the time being. As for the other departments, I can see no real problems there because, whoever it may be, they will have to work under the same guidelines as you do at present. Now I know the direction you wish to go, I will carry out a more detailed investigation and get back to you. It will be a week or more before we need meet again, and until then let's keep it all to ourselves. The last thing we need to do is ruffle a load of feathers if there is no need to.'

It was well into the afternoon when Donald left, and Allen and I spent the rest of the day catching up on the routine tasks around the office. When I left to go home Allen and I walked to our cars together.

I said, 'I'm going to the gym tonight. Why don't you come as well? It will take your mind off things, and I could do with the company.'

'Good idea – we can meet at the gym and maybe grab a takeaway on the way home. At the moment there seems nothing else to talk about, and when you have to keep it to yourself, I don't know about you, but I find it hard.'

We both had a good workout at the gym, and after showering Allen said he would get the food and meet me back at my apartment. By the time he arrived I had a bottle of wine open and the plates on the table. The food was Indian, very hot and spicy. We ate slowly and sipped the wine and talked about the day.

145

In the end he said, 'We've been too successful for our own good. In fact, I thought we could go along forever just as we were. But the thought of covering the Continent frightens me to death.' And I had to agree with him.

He then asked, 'What will you do if it all goes through?'

I had not even given it a thought. 'There are people I want to see and places I've always wanted to visit. But in the long-term, nothing comes to mind. Like you, our company as it is now was, as far as I was concerned, complete. The thought of making it ten or twenty times bigger never entered my mind. Now we have made up our minds, let's see how Donald gets on with the rest of his investigations, and we will go on with things as if nothing has happened for the time being.'

20

After that Donald would ring twice a week with progress reports while Allen and I tried to carry on with the running of the office in the usual manner. It was almost three weeks before Donald asked for another meeting face to face. He said, 'I think it would be better if we held it away from the office, perhaps you could find a small conference room at one of the hotels. If you can make it for Friday, I'll stay over for the weekend and have a look around Oxford.'

There was a good hotel about a mile from my apartment. I rang them and managed to get a room for Friday afternoon, and booked Donald in for the Friday and Saturday nights. When Friday came, after meeting up with Donald we went into a small conference room, although with just the three of us there it seemed huge.

Once we were seated Donald got straight down to business. The first folder contained all the information on the company in Mannheim and he confirmed that the figures he had given us at his last visit were correct. 'The other party in Antwerp was a bit more cagey; they could not make out how I came to know that they were interested in your company. But in talking to them it looks that they would be willing to pay more than the twenty million on offer from Germany. How much more I can't say – they're keeping that close to their chests.

'The next two folders relate to two companies in the Private Health Providers market. Both show interest and both have the resources to purchase your concern. One is based in America but has health facilities operating in this country. The other is based in this country and is active in many different countries. It would appear that they have been looking at your enterprise for over a year, and I think that it will be they who will eventually pay you the money. Being British-based, they already know the data protection laws. The acquisition of your company will benefit the day-to-day running of their existing commitments, and I can see no trouble with the Government departments or, if they still wish to join the register, the armed forces.' He sat back in his chair. 'Well, what do you think?'

Allen and I had been taking notes all the time Donald had been talking; he indicated that I should go first. 'The last option seems to be the best, especially as they are based in this country. If they were to make an offer, how long would it be before they would want to take over? And another point is, would they take on our existing staff and the commitments we have to them?'

'As far as existing staff is concerned, I would think that they will keep them all if they want to stay. They know how the operation is run, and the new people will want their expertise. Your pension scheme and working arrangements look to me to be the same as theirs, so that should be no problem. As to when they would take over running the company, that is more difficult to say – it could be as little as one month or as long as three.'

Donald then asked Allen if there was anything he would like to ask.

'If it goes ahead and they take us over, will they expect Jack and I to stay on to effect the changeover? I for one would not care to stay on after we sell, and I don't think Jack would be very happy either. The day they hand over the money should be the day we leave. It would be better

148

if they gave a commitment to purchase, paid a deposit then send their people in for two weeks prior to the final settlement. This would be time to ease them into the running of things.'

Donald made notes of everything we had said and began to pack away the papers on the table. 'One other thing that I should ask is whether you would want payment all in cash, or would you be willing to take part of the payment in shares in their company?' Allen and I both agreed that a clean break would suit us best.

'Right then, now that we have got that all sorted out, perhaps both of you will join me for dinner. I would rather not eat alone.'

Allen said, 'I've already arranged to go out later and would like to get on my way, but don't let me stop you two.'

I said, 'I'll go home and shower and get into a change of clothes, and then meet you in the dining room at eight.'

Getting back to my apartment I ran a hot bath, and lying with the water up to my chin I let the tension of the day seep out of my body. Afterwards I put on a simple black dress and wore the gold and diamond cross that Daddy had given to me. Looking in the mirror I was pleased with the effect: all the exercise that I had been doing had been worth while.

When I walked into the hotel dining room Donald was seated at the small bar with a single malt at his elbow. He had changed into another suit, and it struck me again that he should be in another type of employment. As he came to greet me, I could not help thinking he should be a vet.

We were shown to a table by the window, and looking out we could see the sleepy spires of Oxford rising above the rooftops. After we had ordered and he had chosen a bottle of wine from the list, he said, 'No more business tonight; you just relax and enjoy your meal. You can start by telling me the things that I should see over the weekend.'

While we were eating I talked about Oxford and the surrounding countryside. I mentioned Woodstock and Blenheim Palace, and the Churchill connection. He said he would enjoy going there, and before I realized it I had offered to take him there tomorrow. 'It will have to be in the afternoon because there are things I must do in the morning.'

'That's fine with me; it will give me time to look around the city before lunch, and then find some fresh air in the afternoon.'

I then turned the conversation round to him. 'You obviously come from a Scottish family, but do you originate from Scotland or were you born here?'

'That's a long story, but yes, I was born in Scotland and was educated there. Father always expected me to go into what he calls the family business. After university I took a degree in Estate Management and Accountancy, which was to set me up for the life he had in mind for me. I wanted to see a bit more of life before settling down to the life that had been planned for me, so I applied and got the position that now pays my day-to-day bills. Just what the future holds I could not say, but I expect the old place will call me back one day.'

It was eleven o'clock when we walked out to the car park. As I unlocked the door he patted the roof and said, 'I like the car.' I looked at the little VW Polo, which was now getting a bit old, and told him that Daddy had bought it for me and I had never thought of changing it. 'If I did trade it in, the next one might be more trouble than it's worth.'

He laughed and said, 'That sounds like Dad and his

car: if it's not broke, don't fix it. I will see you tomorrow afternoon.' With that I drove back to my apartment.

The afternoon at Blenheim Palace was a great success. After walking around the rooms in the house and then the formal gardens, we walked down the long grass walkway that leads from the front of the house to the monument that stands on a rise in the distance. Donald strode out with long strides, and more than once I had to tell him to slow down. He said that he had his training walking through heather on the mountains, this was just a little stroll.

When we eventually returned to my car, I drove straight back to his hotel. He thanked me for a wonderful afternoon and for taking the time to show him around. Just before I left Donald said that from now on he would be in touch with us most days, and he would be there to guide us through the maze of negotiations: 'After all, that's what you're paying me for.' He thanked me again and I watched him as he walked into the hotel. I was surprised that after all that walking and fresh air, I did not sleep well that night.

21

For the next six weeks work went on the same as usual. Allen and I had decided to tell Linda what was happening, but the rest of the staff had no idea what was on the cards. Linda was very special to me, and I wanted her to be the first to know that we intended to sell, and to ensure her that her place in the organization was guaranteed. After all the help she had given me, not only at work but also in my private life, I wished I had given her part of the company.

Donald would talk to me or Allen at least twice a week, and he said that all was going well. We had also had a meeting at the hotel with the top management of the company wishing to purchase our concern. They had raised no objections to the conditions we had laid down concerning the staff; in fact, they indicated that all our existing staff would be offered all their benefits as well as the ones their own staff received at the moment; this included free health care.

They agreed that at least two of their people who would eventually be in charge of our enterprise should have two weeks' instruction on our day-to-day working and to get to know the staff they would be working with. Donald asked for ten per cent of the purchase price before this could happen, and to this they also agreed. All the papers were drawn up and gone over by the solicitors, and the deposit was in the hands of Mr Stroud.

Ann Gibson and Bob Coleman arrived at nine on

Monday; they had been found houses in Oxford, so it looked that they were there to stay. Allen and I enjoyed showing them how everything worked, how the records were kept and retrieved, all the checks that were made on applicants before they were entered on the register, and the security that surrounded the filing system leaving the employees with information on a need-to-know basis, the accounts department and the billing system we employed, and the day-to-day security of the office at all times. After the first week Bob said he could understand why nobody had ever gained access to our records. I told him that if they wanted to continue, their security would have to be as good if not better.

The last week was a strange affair, with Ann and Bob now doing the things that Allen and I had been doing every day for what seemed a lifetime. On Friday morning Allen and I cleared our personal effects. When they were all stored in the back of our cars we drove to Mr Stroud's office to sign the final paperwork and pick up the remainder of the purchase amount.

Mr Stroud had prepared two cheques, one for me and one for Allen. We thanked him for all his help, and as we left he said to me that my Daddy would have been proud of me. Allen then drove me to the bank where we both deposited our cheques. I checked that everything was in order, and that our business account would be closed after the named accounts had been paid.

We then drove back to the office for the last time, this time to say goodbye to all the people we had come to regard as friends. I had an envelope for each of them and wished them well with their new employers. When we left the building I was in a flood of tears. Allen asked, 'What's wrong?'

'Less than five years ago I arrived at that office with a handful of ballpoint pens, and now we are walking away with millions of pounds. I think I have the right to cry a little.'

I spent the next week doing things that needed to be done. And I rang Donald and invited him out for dinner to thank him for all he had done. I offered to go up to town, but he asked if I would book him into the same hotel he stayed in the last time he was in Oxford. He would arrive on Friday night and stay the weekend, and we arranged to have dinner on Friday night and spend Saturday touring around the countryside.

I went to see Linda and explained the arrangements that had been put in place for her: her little house was paid for, so a fund had been set up so she could retire early and live in comfort in her retirement when that time came. We promised to keep in touch and to call on each other if ever the need arose.

On Friday morning I had a meeting with the financial advisers who dealt with my investments. I wanted to find a safe and profitable place to put the money now sitting in my bank. They talked me through all the options, and in the end I told them I was entirely in their hands, as I could see very little difference and each one would give about the same return. They asked, 'How much money will you need transferred to your personal account each month to cover living expenses?'

'I haven't given it a single thought. I've always lived from the wages paid to me by my company. In fact, I had still saved some money in a deposit account up until last week; it's something I've always done.

'Four thousand a month would suit me fine, although I may need a bit more for a start because I'm thinking of buying a new car.'

That's when they told me that after the taxes were paid

154

on the sale of the business, the returns on investments would amount to in excess of ten thousand pounds a week, and that the original investment had grown by nine hundred thousand pounds since it had been made: 'And that is after tax; you must remember you have never drawn a penny from the fund.'

We decided on a figure that I thought I should never need, and left their office more than a little lightheaded.

22

I had dinner that night with Donald at the hotel and thanked him for all he had done for us, and the way that he had done it with so little fuss.

'That's what they pay me for, and believe me, I have been well paid. Up to now the sale of your father's business was the largest negotiation I had handled, but this tops that by some way. I'm just glad it all went according to plan and that I have happy people on both sides of the fence.

'There is one loose end, but only in my own mind. You can tell me it is none of my business and I shall understand, but I have to ask.

'You were the sole owner of the company for a long time, then Allen received five per cent of the company. I wondered why.'

'That's a long story and involves part of my life that I am trying to forget. But if I tell you it may help me, as well as setting your mind at rest.'

'Look, you do not have to tell me anything. Forget I asked.'

'No, I think I should tell you, but let me finish before you ask any questions.'

I started with the evening trip to the theatre, the kidnapping and rape. How after the trial I had locked myself away in the apartment and had not seen anyone face to face for six months. 'If it had not been for Allen, the company would not have survived, and it was he who helped me back into the real world. All that time he didn't ask for anything to cover all the extra hours and the added responsibility he had to shoulder. When I returned to work, I found the business expanded and running smoothly. The five per cent I gave him was in appreciation for his loyalty and hard work. I can't think of anybody who deserved it more.'

Donald listened in silence, and then said, 'I remember reading about the case in the papers at the time. It must have been months of hell. I can see why you gave Allen a share now, but wonder how many people would have done the same. Thank you for telling me; it must have been hard.'

'I'm glad I did. Now let's get back to the present. Tell me where you go, now that you have made me a very rich woman.'

'Now your sale has gone through I intend to go back up to Scotland to see Mother and Father and see what they are up to. Although I keep in touch with them every week, I have not been back to the old pile for nearly two years. I shall enjoy the solitude of the hills and rivers after the hustle and bustle of London. I am not sure that I will be coming back; perhaps it is time for me to help with the running of things up there. But enough about me – what are your plans, or is it too soon to ask?'

'I shall go back to Ethiopia for about six months to see the friends I have still working out there, but that will take a little while to set up. When I return, that will be the time to find a house in the country, and after that, who knows?'

On Saturday morning I dressed in sensible clothes and walking shoes. When Donald arrived I took over the driving and headed west on the A420 and then onto the A338 and made our way towards Wantage and into the Vale of the White Horse. I turned off the country lane onto a single-track road, which took us up to a car park. There were already cars parked and people heading up towards the top of the Downs. And as we started on our way up the sun came out but there was still enough breeze to fly a few kites that fluttered in the sky.

Donald was in his element, and after inspecting the horse carved into the chalk we walked up to the old earth fort on the top of the Downs. Sitting on the grass we looked out over the valley, which seemed to go on forever. I said, 'Do you realize that the last time I sat up here I was twelve and Mum and Daddy sat just down there with a picnic, and it was me who was flying a kite.

'I can't believe I am still so near London.'

Next we headed towards Lambourn and through the Valley of the Race Horse. We stopped at the Swan at Streatley for lunch and looked across the water at the boats waiting to pass through the lock and at the water tumbling down over the weir. With the sun shining on the water, there was no better place to be.

The next stop was Wallingford and I showed Donald where I had lived with Mum and Daddy. He did not mind when I said that I would like to call into the church. We bought some flowers before going, but I was surprised to find flowers already beside the plaque. I lay mine beside them and told Donald that I could not pass through without coming in. The years had passed, but being here still made me cry. It was getting late, so I headed back towards Oxford, where we had dinner at a small country pub.

'That's the best day out I can remember,' he said. 'Without you as a guide, how does anyone ever find the joys we have seen today? Perhaps we should have taken a camera, but then again it's probably better if we just remember the places we have been and the things we have seen.'

158

I dropped him at his hotel, and he thanked me again for a wonderful day and said he would be leaving early next day to go back up to town.

Planning the trip to Ethiopia took up most of the following week. I had written to Kimberly Thornton and told her to expect me in about eight weeks. Linda promised to come in to my apartment twice a week to keep a eye on things and sort out the mail.

On Friday evening I was just thinking what to have for dinner when the phone rang. I picked it up and heard Donald's voice asking how the preparations for my trip were going.

'They're going well; in fact, all that's left to do is get on the plane in seven weeks' time.'

'That might work out well. You see, I am going up to see my family next week, and although it's late in the day I wondered if you might like to accompany me. I shall fly up Monday afternoon and come back the following Monday. With luck and fine weather I shall be able to show you the countryside around my old homestead.'

It cannot be denied that I had thought about last weekend and our time together. But this invitation had come completely out of the blue. I found myself saying, 'What will I need in the way of clothes? And where will we stay? Two days is not long to get myself ready.'

'Nothing grand,' came back the answer, 'something warm and good walking shoes. Mother will get rooms ready, and there is plenty of space for both of us. There will be a few things I have to see to, but that should not take very long. What do you say? Do I tell them you are coming or not?'

'Yes, I would love to come. Shall I drive up to a hotel by the airport and you pick me up there?'

'You will do no such thing: I will stay at that hotel in Oxford on Sunday night and pick you up at your door

159

on Monday morning. That was not so bad was it? I will be with you at eight on Monday – and thanks.'

The phone went dead and I was left staring at the wall.

On Monday morning Donald was quiet on the journey to the airport and seemed to be deep in thought. When we boarded the plane to Aberdeen he started to tell me about the place he called home.

'It's a big old house with a large estate of unproductive land; you have to be a mountain goat to reach most of it. In the distant past, one of my ancestors was given it for service to the crown. And the family has lived there ever since. Twelve years ago Dad found the he could no longer afford to keep it all going, so he moved into the West Wing and leased the main part of the building for fifteen years to a concern who turned it into a hotel. The income from the building was used to help keep the estate together.

'Dad and two old boys look after the grouse, the fishing and the deer, which the hotel guests use at a fee of so much per gun, and so much per rod. Both the shooting and fishing are good and return a good profit. He also runs deer-stalking trips, although no deer are killed. The stalkers carry what look like guns, they even feel like guns, but the only thing they shoot are photographs. Even this has become popular. Now Dad tells me that things are beginning to go wrong again, and he cannot understand why. The trouble is he will not talk about personal money matters to strangers; that's why I'm on my way to see him.'

Donald picked up a rental car when we landed, and it was not long before we were heading down the A93 to Banchory and Crathie. We passed Balmoral Castle and headed towards Braemar. Here Donald turned off the main road and drove along steep narrow lanes. I could see mountains in the distance and Donald told me they

160

were the Cairngorm Mountains and we were nearing the end of our journey.

We turned in through a large stone archway where the iron gates stood open, with large boards advertising the Cairngorm Mountain Hotel on either side. The gatehouse to one side looked as though it was no longer used. As the car climbed up the driveway the roof of the house began to come into view over the top of the rise.

When we reached the top of the rise the house – if it could be called a house – was huge; I would have called it a mansion. To the right was a car park with around thirty cars parked and room for twice that number. We went to the left which led to the West Wing in which Donald's parents lived and we were to stay. Just the West Wing was four times bigger than the house where I grew up, but it all looked tired and in need of attention.

As the car came to a stop a door opened and his parents came out to meet us. Donald's mother was a plump woman a good six inches shorter that he was, dressed in a dark brown skirt and a thick woollen cardigan, her almost white hair pulled back to reveal a smiling round face. Her joy at having him home was plain to see as she came to give him a huge hug.

His father, in cord trousers and heavy working shirt, was the same height as Donald. He came to shake Donald's hand and say it was good to have him home. Looking at me he said, 'Now who have we here?'

'This is Miss North, a recent client and very good friend of mine. She was good enough to show me the sights around her home, so now I'm returning her hospitality.'

They took us into the house and up to the rooms we would be using. His mother said, 'You must want to freshen up after the long journey. When you are ready we shall be in the kitchen, so you just make yourself at home. I have prepared a meal, but take your time, there is nothing to spoil.' When she had gone I sat on the bed and gazed at the massive, freshly polished furniture that filled the large room.

I changed into a light cream dress and black low-heeled shoes and went down to find them in the kitchen. Mrs McNee was bending over the pots on the Aga and the table had been laid with four places, even though it would have seated eight down each side. 'Come on in and take a seat; the others are just on their way and everything is all ready to serve.'

The meal was good plain cooking and finished off with apple crumble and custard. I had not realized I was so hungry and enjoyed everything that was placed in front of me. We sat drinking tea and chatting about the journey. After a while Donald and his father went off to the study, and Mrs McNee started to clear the table and I helped. 'Sit yourself down,' she said, but did not argue when I continued to take things to the sink.

We pulled two winged chairs up near the Aga and she said, 'Now Miss North, what do you do for a living?'

'Well, for a start my name is Jackie. Donald has just sold my business for me and I am off to Africa in seven weeks' time to see friends. After that I really have no idea; I shall just have to wait and see. If I am to stay with you for a week, what would you like me to call you? It seems very formal to call you Mrs McNee all the time.'

'You call me Ma, the same as everyone else around here, and Angus is Donald's father.'

It was getting late and Ma made two mugs of steaming cocoa. I asked, 'Shall I take some to the menfolk, or should I call them?'

'No, my dear, they will be in before long: Angus is always in bed before eleven, so they will be here in a minute.' And as if by magic they both walked through the door, Donald with a worried frown on his face.

162

When the cocoa was finished Donald's parents excused themselves and went to bed, leaving Donald and me seated in the kitchen. He said, 'Sorry about that, but things are a great deal worse than I was led to believe. Now it looks as though I shall be here for a long time. Dad may even have to sell the estate. And if it comes to that, I'll have to stay here to see to all the arrangements. I've been through the figures quickly, but he still won't tell me how much capital he has tucked away on deposit– that's if there is any left at all. But it is a complete mess. I don't know about a short holiday – I may be asking for help before the week's out.'

'If it's as bad as you say, let's get some sleep: we can be up early, and if it's fine we will go for a walk first and then come back for a late breakfast. From then on we will bury ourselves in paperwork and see what we can do. I have no doubt you have your laptop and calculator, your father must have pens, paper and the phone, so what more could you want? Let me tell you, I did Business Management and Accountancy at Oxford University, so between us nothing is impossible.' He grinned and put out the light and we went up to our rooms.

I was up and dressed by half-past six the next morning, but when I went into the kitchen I found Ma and Donald already there. Angus had had his breakfast and gone to check on some stretches of river that were being fished that day, and must have been up at five or before. I smiled at Donald dressed in his walking gear and as he handed me a mug of tea he said, 'What are you grinning at?'

'Now I know why you look out of place down south; you don't belong there. When are you going to realize you belong here, and stop messing about?'

We climbed up through the heather behind the house, and after a while I could see down into and across a large valley. A good mile away, clustered at the foot of the next mountain, were what looked like houses with a small lake nearby. I asked, 'Does anyone still live there? If so it must be lonely in the winter, and where do the people work?' Donald gave me his field glasses, and I could see that the roofs were mostly gone and that it had been deserted for a long time.

'When I was small,' he said, 'families lived there; they were estate workers. But it must be twenty years since the last of them left. There are several places like that on the estate, but none are in use now. The two men that are still working here live in a couple of little cottages attached to the outbuildings near the house.'

'But how many acres does the estate cover? Those buildings over there must be over a mile away.'

'I'm not quite sure; I think one and a half thousand. And Dad thinks he can run it with two men who should have retired five years ago. I bet he has not set eyes on most of it for years. Now you begin to see the problem I have in front of me.'

I said, 'Come on, let's get to it,' and we started back down to the house.

I cried off on the porridge but enjoyed the bacon and eggs (Donald had both), and we then took coffee into the study. There were papers laid out on a table and a large roll-top desk overflowing with papers. He said, 'I think there are twelve years' records here, and the filing system seems to have broken down. What you see on the table I sorted out last night, but as you see, there is some way to go.' I did not know whether to laugh or cry, so I asked where he wanted me to start.

We sorted things into years and months, then into incoming and outgoing. There were ledgers for each year, but nothing seemed to cross-check with the paperwork we had. By mid-afternoon we had twelve piles, with the ledger for each year placed on top of each pile to keep it all in order. Ma brought in tea and sandwiches and looked shocked at the order we had brought to the room. 'It hasn't looked this tidy in years! He won't be able to find a thing.'

When she was gone, Donald said, 'We need to find out what is happening to the income first, and why there seems to be nothing left.' He took years one and eleven, I had years two and ten, and we began to go through them.

It was not long before we looked at each other and Donald said, 'Oh my God! Do you see what I see? It's no wonder there is nothing left – the bastards have been robbing him rotten for years, and he still doesn't know.'

We started to make notes and comparisons of the figures. There were not only the rents for the building, but also the fees for the guns and rods using the estate. In the early years I found copies of the planning and building regulations regarding the conversion of the building to a hotel, copies of the fire chief's reports and recommendations, and copies of building and contents insurance policies which had been forwarded by the hotel management. For the remaining years there was nothing. Donald said, 'I wonder if the building is now insured; it might be an oversight and the following copies were never sent. We haven't found the original lease document, but it must be here somewhere; I'd dearly like to have a read of that.'

It was now early evening and dinner would soon be ready. Donald said that we needed to speak to his Dad before we could go much further; anyway it was time to freshen up before the evening meal.

I asked him, 'Where do we go from here?'

'There are people we need to see and documents I need to read. I shall have to get written authorization from Dad or they won't give me what I need. I'll have

165

another talk to him tonight, then we'll make another start tomorrow.'

It was past six o'clock when I heard the old Land-Rover pull up by the outbuildings; Angus had been out for more than twelve hours. I knocked on Donald's door and we went down to the kitchen. Ma had the table laid, and the pots were steaming on the Aga.

'Dad's late,' said Donald as we walked in.

'No, it's about his normal time; he'll be in in a minute. Sit yourselves down and I'll dish up.'

After the meal Angus and Donald went off to the study, and when the dishes were seen to, Ma and I sat in the winged chairs by the fire again. She sat in silence for a time and then said, 'How bad is it? He does not tell me much, but I know something is very wrong.'

'It's too early to tell. Donald is talking to his Dad now, and if Angus agrees with what Donald wants to do, we will know a lot more by tomorrow night.'

Several times during the evening we heard raised voices coming across the hall from the study. When they eventually came into the kitchen Angus carried a bottle of whisky and two glasses, which he put on the table between them. They looked grave and drank several glasses before Angus rose and told Ma it was time for bed. When they had gone, Donald came and sat with me by the fire.

'Dad and I are going to Banchory tomorrow – he's agreed to let me see the family solicitor, and from there we'll go to the bank. You'll have to stay here with Ma; he wouldn't let me take you with us and still has the idea that outsiders should not be involved in the financial affairs of the family. I now know that there is some capital left; it appears it is in my name, but I won't know how much until tomorrow.' He poured two more whiskies and put water in one of them and gave it to me. We sat in silence for half an hour before going up to bed.

When breakfast was over I left the house and walked past the old Land-Rover and the outbuildings. This time I was heading north and the scenery was different from yesterday. Soon I was walking beside a shallow but fast-flowing stream; where I stopped to gaze into the crystal clear water I could see the fish gliding along around the rocks.

After an hour walking I came to the first of the fishermen I was to see that morning; I saw eight or ten as I continued along the bank. Most were lost in what they were doing and never gave me a second glance, but one or two said 'Good morning,' and one showed me some excellent fish he had already caught. I turned west, and after an hour south to bring me back to the house. There was a worn path leading in that direction, and I followed it because it was easy walking. By the time the house came into view I had met four groups of walkers heading towards the hills in the distance.

Ma was glad to see me back. 'You've been gone all morning, and I was beginning to think you were lost.' She made a pot of tea and we sat by the fire. She said that Angus had never discussed financial matters with her, even though she had asked. 'You know more than I have ever known – won't you try to explain what has happened?'

'This will probably get me in trouble with Angus, but I can tell you what Donald and I have found. When he leased the main building, the amount of rent was very low. The most likely reason was because it would have been at least a year before they would see a return owing to the expense of the internal alterations that had to be made. Donald and I both think that the rent should have at least doubled for the second year, and have increased by at least seven or eight per cent each year after that. It never happened, and the increase amounts to about two or three per cent each year.

167

'The concessions that the hotel guests use on your estate, such as shooting, fishing and deer-stalking, are paid to the hotel and then passed on to you. The amount you receive no way reflects the amount paid to the hotel by their guests – and in the last two months you have received nothing. In truth it surprises me that Angus still has any capital left at all. Donald and his father have gone to the solicitor to get a copy of the original lease, and then on to the bank to find out the state of things there. We'll know more when they get back.'

'Angus is a good man, but when it comes to money he will not tell anybody anything; he sorted out the terms and had his solicitor draw up the paperwork. When it comes to running a business I'm afraid he is still a child, and it doesn't surprise me that he has been made to look a fool. One good thing is that some money was deposited in Donald's name soon after he was born, and he gets it when he takes over the estate. Angus never told me how much it was, but at least it is still there. Then there is the timber that covers a lot of the estate; that must be worth quite a bit. But as I say, he's never discussed the estate business with me.'

23

It was gone four o'clock before Angus and Donald came back from town. They both sat at the table with grave expressions and had the tea and sandwiches that Ma had prepared for them. I was grateful that she did not ask how they had got on. When he had finished eating, Donald said he would like to go for a walk and asked if I would go with him.

As soon as we were away from the house he started to tell me about his day. At the solicitors he had read the original lease that had been drawn up by his father, and at his insistence it had been written up as per his instructions. After that Angus had seen – or not seen – to its implementation. The first year the company was to pay fifty per cent of the yearly rent so the alterations could be carried out and the hotel could start making money. After that the rent would be fixed by an independent valuation of the hotel's turnover and profitability.

'As we now know, none of this ever happened. The rent paid stayed at the first year's figure, and increased by around three per cent a year ever since. The concessions the guests use have been paid on roughly the same principle. The Old Chap has no idea how many use the estate; he just accepts whatever they tell him. When I pointed out he had not been paid anything for two months, he said it had been a poor year and things had been tough on them, but he was sure that payment would be along soon.

'Next was the bank manager. I had a hell of a job to get Dad to let me see all the figures of the estate dealings, and it was even worse when it came to his personal money. With the little income received from the hotel and the other incomes from the estate, I estimate everything will be gone in two years.

'While at the bank I did find out one thing. When I was a year old, five hundred thousand pounds was put on deposit and I was to receive it when the time came for me to take over the estate. The bad news is that Dad insisted that it was held in a deposit account with instant access at the bank, and it has attracted little or no interest from the time it was placed there, even though the bank has advised him to move it many times.'

We went for lunch, but neither of us ate very much. He said, 'If things go on the way they are, there'll be nothing for me to take over. It was hard to talk to him like that. You see, I'm part of the problem: I should have been here looking after things, not gadding off down south, thinking just of myself. In the end he came to a decision, and we made our way back to the solicitors.

'For good or ill, you are now looking at the owner of all you survey, Dad made it all over to me this afternoon. Just what I shall do with it remains to be seen, but I shall have a good try to get it back on an even footing. I had forgotten just how much I love this place, and it would break Dad's heart to lose it. I shall write my resignation tonight; I'll have to go back to see to the sale of the flat, but from now on this will be my home.'

We were sat in the heather looking across the valley at the derelict homes we had seen earlier. The sun was going down, and the heather glowed with its fading light. Donald held my hand as though he needed reassurance. We sat there until the light was almost gone then walked back to the house, still holding hands.

170

The evening meal was a strange affair, with nobody knowing quite what to say. Then Donald asked his Dad if he had told Ma what had happened while they were out during the day. Angus looked at him and told him he would in his own good time. Donald said, 'That time is now; the sooner you get it over with, the better for all of us.' I excused myself and went up to my room so they could talk without me being there.

When I came down later Angus and Ma were in the chairs by the fire, each with a glass of whisky in their hands. Donald came to me carrying two more glasses and took me into the study. 'That is the hardest thing he has ever had to do in his life. Not the fact that he made the estate over to me, but that he had got it all wrong, mainly because he refused to listen to others or take their advice. It will be some time before it really sinks in, and in the end I think he will be happy to let go.'

It was late when we went back into the kitchen; the pair of them were still seated by the fire. I asked if they wanted cocoa, but Angus said he was off to his bed. When he had gone upstairs, Ma came and gave me a hug. 'Thanks for that little chat this afternoon; it helped no end. He now understands that giving the estate to Donald was the only thing he could do, but he wants to end his days where he has lived since he was born.' She gave me a kiss and said how much harder it would have been for her if I had not been there. Donald said, 'That makes two of us,' and went back to making the cocoa.

As we sat sipping the hot drinks he asked when I would be going home. 'There is so much to do, and I could do with some help; if you could spare the time, there is nobody I would rather have on board.' It was an invitation I had hoped for but not expected. I told him that my trip to Africa was not essential; the main reason for going was to take items out with me that I knew were needed.

These could just as well be sent out without me going with them.

Donald then spoke of all the things that were running through his head, like taking back the hotel and running it in conjunction with the estate. 'With the facilities we have here, it could be one of the finest hotels in Scotland. It's not something that will happen overnight, but with hard work and a long-term commitment I'm determined that it will work.'

It was now very late, and as we were putting the mugs into the sink I asked if the long-term commitment included me. He stood there looking at me, not knowing where to put his hands and said that he could never expect me to get so involved. He had nothing to offer but hard work, and a future that was at best uncertain.

I told him it sounded good to me, and if he was offering then I was accepting.

He kissed me for the first time. I said, 'There's no going back now, but what on earth will Angus and Ma say when we tell them? He'll think I am after your money, when all I really want is their son.'

'It's just something else they will have to get used to. But I don't think it will take them long.'

As we reached the landing at the top of the stairs I whispered to him, 'Your place or mine?' He pulled me through the door to his room, but there was little sleep that night.